"Let's cuddle,"

Sandy suggested.

"Later," Wade said quickly. If she regained her memory and awoke to find him in the same bed, she was likely to have him arrested, considering the mutual animosity left over from their divorce proceedings.

Don't think about that, he lectured silently. *It's over. Done. Nothing either of us can ever do will change that, so we may as well stop wishing.*

Wade watched her eyelids droop as sleep overtook her once again. Long dark lashes dusted a shadow over her soft cheeks. Unbidden, Wade's hand cupped her cheek, caressed it. There was a time when his wife had seemed like the perfect mate, the perfect woman. Looking at her lying there, so innocent and at peace, it was easy to forget the bad things and remember all the good.

It was also dangerous and foolhardy....

Dear Reader,

What happens when six brides and six grooms wed for *convenient* reasons? Well... In Donna Clayton's *Daddy Down the Aisle,* a confirmed bachelor becomes a FABULOUS FATHER—with the love of an adorable toddler...and his beautiful bride.

One night of passion leaves a (usually) prim woman expecting a BUNDLE OF JOY! In Sandra Steffen's *For Better, For Baby,* the mom-to-be marries the dad-to-be—and now they have nine months to fall in love....

From secretarial pool to wife of the handsome boss! Well, for a while. In Alaina Hawthorne's *Make-Believe Bride,* she hopes to be his Mrs. Forever—after all, that's how long she's loved him!

What's a rancher to do when his ex-wife turns up on his doorstep with amnesia and a big, juicy kiss? In Val Whisenand's *Temporary Husband,* he simply "forgets" to remind her that they're divorced....

Disguised as lovey-dovey newlyweds on a honeymoon at the Triple Fork Ranch, not-so-loving police partners uncover their own wedded bliss in Laura Anthony's *Undercover Honeymoon....*

In debut author Cathy Forsythe's *The Marriage Contract,* a sexy cowboy proposes a marriage of convenience, but when his bride discovers the real reason he said "I do"— watch out!

I hope you enjoy all six of our wonderful CONVENIENTLY WED titles this month—and all of the Silhouette Romance novels to come!

Regards,

Melissa Senate
Senior Editor

Please address questions and book requests to:
Silhouette Reader Service
U.S.: 3010 Walden Ave., P.O. Box 1325, Buffalo, NY 14269
Canadian: P.O. Box 609, Fort Erie, Ont. L2A 5X3

TEMPORARY HUSBAND

Val Whisenand

Conveniently
Wed

ROMANCE™

Published by Silhouette Books
America's Publisher of Contemporary Romance

To Joe—
the man I love more than chocolate-covered marzipan,
or cuddly little puppies, or fresh spring flowers, or
gorgeous sunsets, or anything else in the whole world.
He's one awesome husband!

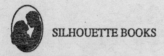 SILHOUETTE BOOKS

ISBN 0-373-19165-0

TEMPORARY HUSBAND

Copyright © 1996 by Val Whisenand

Printed in U.S.A.

VAL WHISENAND

is an incurable dreamer, married to her high school sweetheart since she was seventeen. Her varied interests have led her to explore fascinating occupations and travel throughout the United States, Canada and Mexico. The mother of two grown children, she has lived in Ohio, California and now Arkansas, where the beauty of the countryside and the genuine warmth of the people are a constant joy. The closest town is called Heart. What better place for a romantic to dwell than near to the Heart!

I, Wade Walker,
take you, Sandy Walker,
to be my wife—
at least until you regain your
memory about our divorce.
I promise to go through with this charade—
and try to ignore how incredibly sexy
you look in my bed....

x *Wade Walker*

♥♥♥

I, Sandy Walker,
take you, Wade Walker,
to be my husband—
again!
I promise to
make this marriage work—
despite your odd behavior and
reluctance to go on a honeymoon....

x *Sandy Walker*

Chapter One

Breathing a sigh of absolute relief, Sandy Walker rested her hands on the wheel of her station wagon and momentarily closed her eyes. Lord, her head hurt! But she was home, she reminded herself with a slight smile. Home to her husband, Wade, and the comfort of their wonderful house. It wasn't as big or impressive as the residence she'd grown up in, but it was sure more of a home.

A little stiff, she climbed out of the car, eyeing the crumpled front wheel on her mountain bike as it lay in the back of the wagon. She was darned lucky she hadn't been seriously hurt when she fell. Especially since she hadn't been wearing her protective helmet the way she was supposed to.

Leaving the bike behind, she shouldered her purse and headed up the cement walkway to the front door. All she wanted was a big hug from Wade, a hot bath and some sleep.

Sandy opened the door, stepped inside and called out to her husband. "Honey? I'm home."

In the kitchen, preparing dinner for one, Wade heard her summons clearly. Thinking at first that he was having hallucinations, he froze in midmotion. It had been literally years since Sandy had called out to him that way, and he figured he had to be hearing things.

He continued to stand very still, listening carefully. Nothing. Although he assumed he was simply temporarily mentally unbalanced, he decided it was best to investigate. Laying aside the plate of leftover chicken that was to be his evening meal, he headed for the front of the house.

Broad-shouldered and muscular, yet light on his feet, Wade was thoroughly appealing, from his wavy brown hair all the way to his toes and all parts in between. There was the ever-present spark of excitement in his dark, coffee-colored eyes, too. Sandy trembled in anticipation. That sexy look he was using to scan her from head to foot did the same thing to her libido every time.

His light-blue chambray shirt was unbuttoned and hung loose, its sleeves rolled up to reveal the dusting of dark hair on his forearms. Hurrying to his side, Sandy slid her arms around him beneath the loose fabric and laid her cheek on his bare chest, reveling in the warmth and maleness of his skin. "Oh, boy, am I glad to be here."

Wade scowled down at the young woman clinging so brazenly to his seminaked torso while arguing with himself that he had to be dreaming. It took supreme effort to keep his hands hanging free at his sides. "You are?"

Smiling tenderly, she lifted her gaze to look directly into the square-jawed face she loved so much. "You bet. And stop frowning. I have a pounding headache, but I'm fine."

"Uh, good."

"No kidding. You should see my poor bike! I hope it's not a total wreck. If it hadn't been for the darned wild bunnies, everything would have been okay."

She released him with a brief squeeze and headed down the hall. "What I need now is a nice, hot bath. I was going to take a shower, but my muscles are starting to get pretty sore so I think a soak in the tub would be best.''

Wade overcame his initial shock enough to follow her. No dream was this real. ''A bath?''

''Uh-huh.''

He stopped in his tracks as Sandy entered the master bedroom without a pause. He hadn't seen her act so loving and naturally at home in ages. As a matter of fact, he hadn't seen her at all for about two years! Not that she looked much different. Her light-brown hair was a bit shorter and more flyaway than usual, he guessed, but those hazel eyes of hers were as dangerous to his self-control as ever. So was her body, in spite of the fact she was currently hiding it under a loose-fitting sweatshirt and jeans.

Wade knew he didn't dare allow Sandy back into his life. Losing her the first time had been far too painful. He followed her as far as the doorway to the bedroom. ''Now, wait just a minute.''

''I'd like to stop and talk, but I really am beat,'' she called over her shoulder.

He watched as she lifted the sweatshirt over her head, revealing a lightweight blouse with tiny, pink roses that reminded him sadly of her penchant for the sweet-smelling blossoms.

Smiling, she motioned to him. ''Come on in. Don't be bashful. I said I had a headache, but I can still fill you in on my adventure while I get undressed. I have dried leaves and pine needles in some pretty strange places, believe me.''

Wade grabbed her hands just as she was about to pull the blouse off, as well. ''Hold it, lady. I don't know what your game is or what you're up to, but you're *not* getting undressed in my house, you got that?''

''Don't be silly. It's my house, too, isn't it?''

''No.''

She giggled, her light-headedness and mental confusion making everything he said seem hysterically funny.

"You're cute," Sandy said, reaching up to place a conciliatory kiss on his cheek. "It isn't my fault you didn't want to go riding in the forest with me. You'd have loved Big Bear Lake. The temperature was much cooler up there than it is down here. No smog, either."

His scowl deepening, Wade tightened his hold. "I haven't the slightest idea what you're talking about, Sandra, but I'm not amused."

"You would have been if you'd seen the comedy of errors that knocked me in the ditch," she said with a chuckle. "There was this cute little redheaded boy walking an Irish setter practically big enough for him to ride. They were a matched set, kind of like he'd picked the dog because it looked like him. Anyway, I thought I could get around them on the narrow trail—only the minute that dog saw the wild rabbits, I was a goner."

Rabbits again, Wade thought. And now dogs, too. If his ex-wife figured he was going to buy a crazy, nonsensical story like that she was mistaken. He didn't know what her current game was, nor did he care. Not after everything that had happened in the past. All he wanted to do was get her out of his house and out of his life before he—

The dire consequences of his lascivious thoughts brought him up short. He would *not* allow his sweet, sexy memories of Sandy or her apparent amorousness to get in the way of what he knew he had to do. It didn't matter whether he was strongly attracted to her physically or not, which he certainly was. That feeling was nothing new. He could handle it.

She wobbled on her feet momentarily, then righted herself with a hand on her temple. "Ooh. Good thing you're standing there. I'm a little woozy."

Considering her carefully and noting the paleness of her fair skin, her disheveled appearance and the jagged rip in the elbow of her discarded sweatshirt, Wade felt his resolve weaken a bit, although not enough to make him change his mind.

"You fell off your mountain bike—is that what you're trying to tell me?"

"Of course, silly."

"Have you seen a doctor?"

"No. I'll be fine. Honest. The other folks on the trail were concerned when they saw me hit the ditch, too, but once they'd helped me get the bike back to the car I felt much better." Rubbing her head, she noted a bump the size of a hen's egg on her scalp and winced. "Ouch. I stopped for a soda and took a couple of aspirin on the way home, but my head still hurts like the dickens."

"On the way home?"

"Sure." Sandy laid her cheek against her husband's chest and sighed. "You have no idea how good it feels to be here with you and to know you'll take good care of me. I know I've always been pretty independent, but right now I could use a giant dose of your special TLC."

Cautiously, gently, Wade threaded his fingers through her silky, naturally wavy hair, trying his best not to enjoy the tactile sensation. There was a bump all right, a good-size one, to the right of the midline a few inches back from her bangs.

Okay, he reasoned, absently smoothing her hair as he withdrew his hand. So she had had a mishap of some sort. That was no excuse for coming to him as if they were still married and acting the part of the damsel in distress. If she wanted her damn bicycle fixed she could just take it to a bike shop. As for her head, the sensible thing was to go see a doctor, and he told her so.

"I don't need a doctor nearly as much as I need some rest," she countered.

"You're not supposed to go to sleep right after a head injury. When exactly did this happen?"

"Um…" Sandy was puzzled. "I'm not sure. Some of the details keep going away and coming back. There are a few hours I can't seem to remember at all."

"I'm calling a doctor." Letting her go, he reached toward the telephone on the bedside table, then realized that unless he intended to dial 911, he would have to go into the den to get a phone book and look up the number of a local emergency clinic.

Sandy rubbed her eyes with her knuckles, noticing for the first time that they were skinned, too. "Do whatever you think is best, honey. I'll be in the bathroom."

"You can't go in there alone," Wade cautioned, realizing he'd opened himself up to some embarrassing suggestions the minute the words were out of his mouth.

"I thought you'd never ask," Sandy said, her voice almost a purr. "Want to wash my back?"

"No!"

"Sure you do," she said, gazing up at him and seeing the truth of his desire plainly evident in his expression.

"I'm just concerned about your safety," he alibied. "What if you fall down and hit your head again?"

"There's no problem as long as you're there to catch me." Taking a step backward, she sank heavily onto the foot of the bed and cradled her head in her hands. "Boy, am I beat."

"You can't go to sleep," Wade insisted.

"I know. I just need to lie down and rest for a couple of minutes to get my strength back. Then I can take a bath and wash my hair, okay?"

It was *not* okay. None of this was. He was beginning to feel far too protective toward his injured ex, and that, in turn, was evidently affecting his physical reactions, because his body was more than ready to forget the past and step wholeheartedly into whatever trancelike world Sandy was inhabiting. He had to get rid of her before he did or said something he would be eternally sorry for.

Turning on his heel, Wade stalked out of the room to make the necessary phone call.

As soon as the clinic's receptionist answered, Wade got right to the point. It occurred to him he might have more luck obtaining an appointment if he didn't get too specific about his and Sandra's current marital situation, so he simply avoided it.

"My wife has fallen off her bicycle and hit her head," he said. "I need to bring her in right away."

"Yes, sir. How long ago did this accident happen?"

"Uh, I'm not sure. I didn't witness the fall."

"I see. One moment, please. Let me connect you with Dr. Simmondson."

Uptight about Sandy in spite of their rocky past, Wade felt the short wait for the physician was far too long. When he finally did get the doctor on the line, the man's apparent lack of serious concern and matter-of-fact attitude were not at all comforting.

"Simmondson. How can I help you?"

"As I told the woman who answered the phone, Sandy fell off her bike."

"I see. And who is Sandy?"

"My wife—ex-wife—oh, hell, what difference does it make? She needs to see a doctor."

"Is she conscious?"

Wade nodded. "Yes. She drove home from the mountains by herself."

The doctor sounded even less concerned than before. "What are her symptoms?"

"I don't know exactly. She's been acting crazy."

Simmondson chuckled. "So has my ex. That doesn't mean she needs medical attention."

"There's a bump on her head."

"Where exactly?"

"On the top, to one side of the center. Why?"

"Because there are head injuries and there are head injuries. The location of the trauma can make a lot of difference in its severity. If your wife is conscious and her pupils are equal and reactive, I wouldn't worry about her. A little disorientation is normal."

Wade remembered looking deeply into the golden green depths of Sandy's bewitching eyes, but he'd been so mesmerized by the experience he couldn't be sure both her pupils had been the same size. "How do I tell for sure?"

"Shine a flashlight into her eyes and see if the pupils contract evenly. If they do and the size doesn't become unequal later, you can let her recover on her own."

"She wants to sleep. Isn't that dangerous?"

"Not necessarily. Since you say she drove a car, apparently successfully, it's my guess she's fine. If you're worried, just wake her up every couple of hours and check her eyes."

Wade grimaced. Wake her every couple of hours? That sure precluded taking her home, didn't it? "In case there is a problem later, can I reach you during the night?"

"Someone will be on call, yes. Just tell the nurse you already talked to me and I gave you instructions about what to watch for."

"Okay. Thanks."

Wade hung up the receiver and stood there, thinking. Seeing Sandy again, especially when she so obviously needed him, was causing havoc with his usually staid emotional state, but he supposed one night of caring for her wasn't going to kill him. He couldn't very well deliver her to wherever she was now living and simply dump her there, could he? In her confused frame of mind there was no telling what she would do or where she might go. Besides, who would check on her physical condition during the night if not him?

Maybe she had a roommate, he thought with a surge of relief. Sure. He would call Sandy's place, find out, and if there was someone living with her, ask the person to be waiting for them when he drove her home.

Suppose it was a *man?* Wade asked himself. He made a face. *So what? Who cared?* As long as he got her out of his house and out of his bed, it didn't matter if she was bunking with an entire water-polo team complete with Speedo trunks and bulging muscles.

Not that he was less of a he-man than that, he reminded himself. He worked out with weights almost daily and could hold his own with practically anyone. Except Sandy, he added ruefully.

Grumbling to himself, he walked to the hall table where she had left her purse and looked in it for her wallet and driver's license, returning to the phone as soon as he located her current address.

Ignoring his inner compulsion to abandon the quest for someone else to relieve him of the alluring woman in his bed, he dialed her home number, disgusted at himself for hoping no one would answer.

A generic answering machine message was all the response he got. He hung up and headed back to the bedroom.

Sandy had lain down just where he'd left her, clothes and all, thank goodness. She appeared to be asleep.

The first thing Wade did was slip off her shoes, then her socks. There were pine needles in the cuffs of her socks. Nevertheless, that was the end of the disrobing as far as he was concerned.

Lifting her gently, he drew her all the way onto the comforter and laid her head on a pillow, making sure she was as cozy as possible before covering her with a spare blanket.

Ready for the big California earthquake the local scientists and newspeople kept insisting was imminent, Wade kept a flashlight in the bedside table. He retrieved it and spoke softly to Sandy.

"Wake up. Come on. Open your eyes. I need to look at your pupils."

She made a mewing sound, curled closer to him and reached out. Her eyelids fluttered, then lifted. The moment she focused on his face her lips lifted in a provocative smile. "Hi, honey. You coming to bed soon?"

Wade blushed and fidgeted in spite of the righteous indignation he was trying to nurture. "No, Sandra, I'm not. You hit your head, remember? I called the doctor and he said I should check your pupils. Open your eyes and look at this light."

She tried. "Ooh. That hurts."

"What does?"

"My head. My eyes." She wiggled slightly and grimaced. "Just about every bone in my body."

"Well, you don't seem to have a serious injury," he said, relieved to have seen the naturally healthy reaction of her eyes.

"Good. Then let's cuddle."

"Later," he said, deciding a white lie was better than arguing with her when she was still so confused. If she recovered her senses and awoke to find him in the same bed, she was likely to have him arrested, considering the mutual animosity left over from their divorce proceedings.

Don't think about that, he lectured silently. *It's over. Done. Nothing either of us can ever do will change that so we may as well stop wishing.*

Wade watched her eyelids droop, her breathing slow and even out as sleep overtook her once again. Long, dark lashes dusted a shadow over her soft cheeks. Unbidden, Wade cupped her cheek with his hand, caressed it. There was a time when his wife had seemed like the perfect mate, the perfect woman. As he looked at her lying there, so innocent and so at peace, it was easy to forget the bad things and remember all the good.

It was also dangerous and foolhardy, he added, pulling away and getting to his feet to put more distance between them. He would allow her to spend one night, then ship her off to the hospital if she wasn't better. With Sandy in the house it was far too easy for his heart to command his mind. He had let that happen once, with dire consequences. It wasn't going to happen again.

Chapter Two

Sweet thoughts crowded Sandy's dreams, making her feel warm and loved and safe. Wade was present, of course. He always appeared when she needed him most. He was kissing her, making passionate love to her. Judging by the elegant room and the enormous, round bed they were lying in, it was the first night of their honeymoon.

"Um, I could do that forever," she murmured when he rolled off and sank, exhausted, onto the dusky-rose-colored sheets beside her. Her fingers traced tiny circles in the curly, dark hair on his bare chest, making him shiver.

"I wish *I* could," he said with a weary sigh. "You, lady, are insatiable."

"Oh, look who's talking. I wasn't the one who insisted we had to get married so soon."

"Only because you wouldn't sleep with me otherwise," Wade said teasingly.

"You could have waited till I got my degree, you know."

"Not if I wanted to keep my sanity, honey." He drew her against him and wrapped her in a possessive embrace. "Besides, I intend to show you what it's like to belong to a real family."

"Speaking of which, my mother thinks you're crazy, anyway, so what difference would waiting a few more months have made?"

"That question works two ways, you know. I promised I'd support you in anything you wanted to do and I meant it, even if you decide to go on and get your master's degree. That's more than your parents ever did."

She cuddled closer, her head resting on his shoulder. "True. And I believe you, Wade. It's just that getting a good education means so much to me. I don't want to do anything that might spoil my chances."

"You haven't, honey," he whispered, nuzzling her neck in the process.

"I know. I love you, Mr. Walker."

"And I love you."

Reaching to caress his muscular body in consummate appreciation of its many fine physical attributes, she noted his new arousal and giggled. "I thought you were tired."

"Parts of me are," he answered with a throaty chuckle.

"I just found a part that isn't."

"I know you did. And if you don't stop that, lady, I won't be responsible for my actions."

"Oh, good," she said, her breathlessness lending seriousness to her glib reply.

Then, just as Wade was preparing to take her as his bride once more, he seemed to withdraw, his image fading away, her conscious mind struggling back from the bliss the dream had brought.

Half-asleep, Sandy smiled, rolled over and reached to touch him in the bed beside her. The pillowcase was cold. Smooth and cold to the touch. Her hand groped, fingers spreading, searching, as she slowly came awake. Blinking in the dimness, she managed to focus. Enough light was filtering through from the hallway to show that Wade was clearly missing.

She pushed the blanket back and sat up, realizing at once that she was suffering from a pounding headache and stiff, achy muscles. For a few seconds she simply held still, trying to recall what had happened to make her feel so awful. Flashes of insight darted into her mind, only to be scattered by other, disconnected memories, like a broken strand of pearls hitting a slick floor.

Taking a deep breath, she swung her legs over the side of the bed and stood up, wobbling a bit till she got her balance. Wade would know what was wrong with her, she thought. Obviously he'd been relaxing in front of the television set and had dozed off, as usual. That was why the hall light had been left on.

A slight smile lifted the corners of her mouth. In the early days of their marriage she had been appointed quasi-official sandman, in charge of getting him up and into bed rather than letting him wile away the night on the sofa when TV lulled him to sleep after a hard day's work.

Padding barefoot to the door, she eased it all the way open and stepped out, noting for the first time that she still wore her blouse and jeans. How silly! Well, as soon as she rousted Wade and got him to bed she would remedy that oversight.

She tiptoed quietly into the living room, gazing at him with tenderness and love. He'd removed his shirt and shoes but not his jeans. As suspected, he was sound asleep on the leather couch, his long legs curled up because there wasn't room to fully extend them.

Sandy laid a hand on his shoulder, caressing the warm skin as she whispered, "Honey?"

He didn't respond other than to lick his lips and scowl in his sleep.

Bending over, she placed a tender kiss on his mouth, deepening it as he began to kiss her in return. This was what made everything else in her life worthwhile, she thought, lowering herself to her knees beside the couch and ignoring the discomfort of her earlier injuries. Running her fingers through his hair, she continued to keep her lips pressed hard to his.

Wade's arms came around her then, and she settled her upper torso onto his chest with a heartfelt sigh of contentment. His eyes fluttered open. Sandy smiled. "Hi, sleepyhead."

He jumped away so violently she was knocked off balance, and landed on her rear on the carpet, arms and legs akimbo.

"What do you think you're doing?"

"Putting you to bed," she said, wincing and rubbing her rear end with one hand. "At least, I was trying to."

In seconds, Wade had taken stock of the ironic situation and realized the damage his quick reflexes might have done to her already traumatized body. He dropped to one knee beside her. "I'm so sorry, Sandy. Are you hurt?"

"Not any more than I was, I don't think," she said, flexing her arms and slowly shaking her head. "What happened to me, anyway?"

"You crashed your mountain bike."

"I did?" Blinking to try to clear her head, she frowned. "Why don't I remember doing it?"

"I don't know. You told me all about it when you got here." Wade stood, held out his hand and helped her up. "The doctor said it's normal to be kind of out of touch with reality for a while when you've had a head injury like yours."

Sandy was pressing her fingertips against the throbbing pain in her temples but managed a wry smile anyway. "Then I guess I'm normal, which is not saying a lot, since I seem to have gone to bed with all my clothes on."

She swayed a little from momentary dizziness and felt Wade grasp her shoulders. "Thanks. I didn't think I was this shaky when I crawled out of bed to come get you."

"Is that what you're doing in here?"

"Sure. It's my job, remember? You never did like to be abandoned on the couch when I went to bed."

"Right." Humoring her, he started to guide her toward the only bedroom that was furnished for sleeping.

"I should strip and shower before I get the sheets all dirty," Sandy murmured, speaking mostly to herself.

"That won't be necessary." Wade led her to the side of the comfortable mattress, turned down the covers more fully than he had before and gently pushed her into a sitting position. "Here we are."

"Really, honey, I . . ."

"Don't argue, Sandra. The doctor told me to wake you every couple of hours to check on you anyway, so we might as well do that now." He reached for the flashlight and flicked it on. "Look at me."

"What are you doing?"

That question really bothered Wade. She had made a big deal about the simple test the first time he had performed it only a short time before, yet now she seemed totally oblivious to the details. The longer he kept company with her, the more worried he got.

"I'm looking at your pupils," Wade said. "Just stare at the light and let me see your eyes."

"They're green," Sandy reminded him. "You always said they looked sparkling, as though they had flecks of real gold and emeralds in them, remember?"

Wade grimaced. "Yeah, I remember." Without consciously giving the movement any thought, he cupped her warm cheek in his hand again and gently embraced it while he steadied her head.

She turned her face, cuddled into his palm and kissed it. "Good. Now, if you're finished making like a medic, can we go to bed? I'm bushed."

"Fine. Lie down and close your eyes."

"Oh, no, you don't," she said, her voice a come-hither invitation, her arms reaching to grasp his neck as he leaned down briefly to cover her with the sheet and blanket. "You have to join me."

"You have a headache," Wade reminded her.

"It's not *that* bad."

"As far as I'm concerned, it is," he said, deciding that it would be best to continue to go along with her delusions about their marriage, at least until morning. He reached up and grasped her wrists to disentangle himself. "Close your eyes and get some sleep."

"Um. If you say so." Her voice began to weaken. "But you're missing a great opportunity, mister."

Gritting his teeth, Wade stood over her and watched till he was certain she had drifted off. So innocent. So beautiful. He shook his head. This was *not* real. Oh, it was happening, all right, but he might as well be trapped in some preposterous virtual-reality game.

He checked his watch in the reflected hall light. Five hours till dawn. Good Lord, that was practically forever! Making his way back to the sofa, he stepped out of his jeans and dropped them onto the floor.

Never one to bother with pajamas, he groaned in sexual and mental frustration as he crashed onto the couch. Pulling a spare coverlet over himself, he laid his forearm across his eyes to blot out the hard facts of his current situation. The ploy failed. All he could envision was Sandy, his Sandy, lying in bed and reaching out to him in all innocence.

Any other man would take what she's offering, he told himself. *Even if she doesn't know what she's doing.*

"But I'm not any other man," Wade muttered. "She came to me because she trusts me, and I can't let her down."

He cursed under his breath. Damn, this was going to be a long night!

Wade was roused from his restless sleep by a sound he couldn't readily identify. Then he heard it again, soft but distinguishable. Probably Sandra's headache kicking up, he thought, wondering if he should pull on his pants and go to her to see if she wanted an aspirin.

Rubbing sleep from his eyes, he peered at the glowing face of his watch. Less than an hour had passed since the last time he'd checked her pupils.

He strained to listen, knowing that if he heard much more whimpering his conscience would insist he investigate no matter what the constant contact was doing to his emotional stability.

The house was totally silent. Relieved, he sank back against the barely comfortable toss pillow he'd had his head on and closed his eyes.

Sandy clenched her teeth. *They left me again,* she said to herself, tears of loneliness building behind her eyelids. *Mama and Daddy are gone.*

She could see herself clearly, standing in the center of the enormous great room in the house where she'd grown up. She was wearing her favorite red cardigan and holding her schoolbooks and empty lunch box. The place was spotless, as usual, but that was thanks to a live-in housekeeper, not to Sandy's mother.

Mama was probably "sick" again, she thought, which meant she'd be either in the bedroom suite, sleeping it off, or lying in the sun by the pool, with an icy drink sitting on the deck beside her.

Feeling as if she were floating and walking at the same time, Sandra made her way outside. Everything was pristine here, too, even the flower beds beneath the weeping willow tree that was her favorite place to play hide-and-seek.

"Mama? Are you here?" she called. "I'm home. I got an *A* on my spelling test again!"

But Mama wasn't out there. Neither was Daddy. Concerned, though not really frightened, she accepted her solitary fate as normal and went to the swing hanging from a bare metal framework behind the gazebo. Between drawn-out business trips abroad, her father had finally installed it there, but not before both parents had argued loudly about what the presence of such an ugly children's toy would do to the aesthetics of their carefully manicured landscape.

Sandy pouted. Didn't they see how lonesome she was? Didn't they care? Parents were supposed to care about their kids, weren't they? Maybe if they'd bought her a puppy as she wanted, at least she wouldn't have to be alone all the time.

Pushing her feet against the ground as she closed her eyes, she set the swing in motion and let its even, back-and-forth movement lull away her chronic feelings of familial abandonment.

Suddenly it was dark. And cold. She opened her eyes, jumped from the swing and dashed for the safety of the house. All the doors were locked! Pounding with her fists, she called to someone, anyone, to open up and let her in.

Genuine tears spilled from her eyes, sliding down her temples to wet her hair. It was *scary* out there.

"Mama! Mama, where are you?"

The darkness was closing in, full of unnamed monsters and the ghosts of her past. Why didn't her parents answer? Where had they gone?

Thick and heavy, the very air seemed to press down on her, trapping her in the frightful dream. Again and again she tried to shout for help and was thwarted by an apparent lack of sound. If only she could get them to *hear* her!

Opening her mouth wide and taking the deepest breath she could muster, Sandy screamed.

Wade came up off the couch as if it had suddenly caught fire beneath him. This time he didn't have to stand there and wonder if his unexpected houseguest was okay. It was obvious she wasn't.

He sprang for the bedroom, stumbling over his blanket until he could cast it off. Batting at the light switch in passing, he missed, but ignored the error as he came to rest on the edge of the bed and took her shoulders in his strong but gentle grip.

"Sandy! What is it? What's wrong? Are you worse?"

The instant her eyes opened and she saw him beside her she reached out and grasped him tightly. "Oh, Wade. Thank goodness you're here! I had the most awful nightmare."

He wasn't going to hug her in return. He wasn't. It was just that she seemed so vulnerable, and she was holding on to him so firmly that his arms passed around her of their own accord. Rubbing her back to calm her, he noted she had almost ceased sobbing and was, instead, breathing nearly as rapidly as he was.

"It's okay, honey. You're fine," he said with a lump in his throat. Not that he'd ever let on to Sandra how deeply her presence and neediness were affecting him, however. Oh, no. Confession might be good for the soul, but it was definitely not recommended when a man found his attractive, sexy, former wife in his bed.

"How's your head?" He eased her away from him and searched her expression, hoping thoughts of her injury would defuse the electrifying situation. Thank goodness she hadn't noticed he was no longer wearing his jeans, because there was no way he could hide the prompt and visible physical reaction of his body.

"It hurts," she said, sniffling. "And now my sinuses are killing me, too." She made a silly, cynical face and sniffled while she wiped away her tears. "Terrific, huh?"

Wade had to smile in spite of himself. He had forgotten how Sandy's sense of humor tended to come to the fore whenever things went awry. Which they certainly had, he reminded himself soberly. "What was your dream about?"

"I—I honestly can't remember," she said, looking puzzled. "But I sure wasn't happy, was I?"

"Apparently not."

She sniffled again. "Got a tissue?"

"Sure. Here." He opened the drawer of his nightstand and handed her an entire box. "Keep it."

Overjoyed to awaken and find Wade beside her, she felt lighthearted beyond belief and more than a little capricious. It showed in her retort. "All for me? Wow!"

Wade scowled, unamused. "Business is good. I can afford to be generous."

"I'm glad. How's Art doing, anyway? Is he working out okay in the shop?"

Wade's younger brother had long ago become an indispensable part of his printing business. Sandy should know that. Her outdated comment was just one more indication of how far from reality her mind had strayed.

"Art's fine," he said, watching for any reaction that might indicate normalcy.

She paused to blow her nose and pitch the tissue into the wastebasket. "Good. I told you he would be. He's a great kid. You're lucky to have him as a brother. I always wanted one, you know."

"Yeah, I know."

She laid her hand lightly on his arm, caressing, stroking. "We'll have lots of kids when the time comes, I promise. I love you very much, Wade. You know that, don't you?" When he got a funny look on his face and didn't answer immediately, she added, *"Don't you?"*

Every muscle in his body had tied in an uncomfortable knot, the most painful of which was his heart. He got stiffly to his feet. "Go to sleep, Sandra. We'll talk in the morning."

Moving rapidly enough that she was overcome by a wave of dizziness, she reached out and grasped his hand, stopping him from leaving. "Ooh. Remind me not to try *that* again."

Wade snorted in self-derision. "I suppose I'd better look at your eyes one more time."

"They're still hazel—honest, they are," she assured him. "I'm going to have a sunburned face before morning if you don't stop flashing that stupid bright light at me all the time."

"You can't get a sunburn from a flashlight."

Sandy grinned. "I know that. Don't I get all the biology questions right when we play that TV quiz show game together?"

"Right." Wade was thankful he couldn't find any change in the reactions of her pupils. "You're fine. Just don't try to get up in such a hurry and you probably won't get so dizzy, okay?"

"Okay." She was holding tightly to his wrist and she didn't let go, even when he tried to move away. "Where are you going?"

"Back into the living room."

"Why? Did we have a fight?"

"No."

"Then stay with me. Please?" She managed another brief smile through the fluctuating agony in her throbbing head.

Wade saw the flicker of pain in her gaze. It cut him to the depths of his soul in spite of their troubled past. Nevertheless he shook his head. "You're hurt. I don't want to do anything that might make it worse."

"Get me a couple of aspirin and stop worrying, will you? I'll be fine. I just need my husband to hold me for a bit while I doze off."

Wade gritted his teeth. After her casual comment about children it was obvious she had no idea what had happened. Therefore he knew he shouldn't hold it against her.

At least, not for the present. Besides, he had other concerns, such as trying to ignore the lingering sexual chemistry between them that was about to drive him mad.

He couldn't just pack her off to someplace else, either. Since he wasn't up-to-date on who her friends were, there was clearly nowhere he could send her for the kind of personalized care she presently needed. Not in the middle of the night.

"Please?" she begged, suddenly quite serious.

This was one confrontation Wade's heart told him he wasn't going to win. "It means that much to you?"

"Yes. You have no idea how safe and well I feel when I'm lying in your arms and I can hear you breathing, feel the warmth of your body." She let her gaze wander down his torso and settle on another part of him crucial to their marital relationship. Raising her eyes to his, she added, "And other things, of course."

"Very funny."

"Not usually," she cracked back, "but there have been a few times when things got a little out of hand . . . no pun intended." She giggled and reached for him, but he dodged her nimble fingers.

"That'll be the day," Wade muttered. He made a sour face as he adjusted his shorts for comfort and circled around the bed. "Okay. Shove over and give me a little room. If the only way I'm going to get any sleep is to bunk with you, then that's what we'll do."

"Good." She started to move, then paused with her hand on her forehead. "Ooh. Ouch. How about those aspirin, first?"

Wade nodded, sorry he'd grumbled at her. "Sure. Want to take them with water or orange juice?"

"Orange juice, please."

As Wade left the bedroom she couldn't help admiring his strong physique from the back. His waist was narrow, his legs muscular and dusted with the same dark hair that graced his broad chest...and below. If her head hadn't hurt so much and he hadn't been in such a strange, inhibited mood at the moment, she might have called a ribald compliment after him the way her sense of humor urged her to.

Sandy smiled to herself. Poor Wade. He was trying so hard to be nice to her while she was sick. She could wait for lovemaking if he could, she supposed. Tomorrow, when she could prove to him she was really okay, they would discuss the reasons for his recent standoffish attitude and the lack of intimacy in their marriage lately.

Unless, of course, he grew amorous during what was left of the night. Holding that pleasant thought, she made herself comfortable on the feather pillow and waited for him to return with her aspirin, juice and that body of his that just wouldn't wait.

Chapter Three

Wade was not a happy camper. He'd managed to keep a ridge of bedclothes between their bodies and had put his jeans back on when he went to fetch the aspirin, but nothing seemed to relieve his "problem." Thank goodness Sandy had finally fallen asleep and quit trying to caress him.

As he listened to her even breathing he recalled the compliment she'd given him about feeling safe with him beside her. It did seem right for them to be together like that, didn't it? Preordained almost, which didn't help him maintain the rancor and aloofness he was doing his best to perpetuate.

When she cuddled closer he lifted his arm and put it around her, making her a pillow of his shoulder, then closed his eyes and eventually dozed.

That was the position they were still in when she awoke. Gazing up at him, Sandy smiled. Poor thing. Wade looked really wrung out, and no wonder, considering the ordeal she'd put him through.

"Honey?" she said softly. "Are you awake?"

He merely licked his lips and moaned slightly, making her
yearn to kiss him again no matter how achy and grungy she
felt. Instead she opted for a shower first and slid slowly out
of his embrace, watching to make sure he was not dis-
turbed, then made her way to the spare bathroom down the
hall rather than trying to shower in the one off the master
suite, where Wade slept.

Easing the bathroom door closed behind her, Sandy
started to disrobe. The floor tile and large, crystal mirror
were the same, but the teal-colored, terry-cloth towels
hanging on the towel bar looked terribly faded. She scowled.
Now, when had *that* happened? And why? They hadn't had
those towels more than six months.

Sighing, she shrugged out of the last of her clothing. Oh,
well, what mattered now was getting the forest grime off her
and washing her hair.

Since her favorite hair-care products were kept in the
master bathroom and she didn't want to chance waking
Wade before she'd had time to surprise him with a nice
breakfast, she settled for a bottle of his generic shampoo,
turned on the water and stepped beneath the prickly spray
as soon as it was tolerably warm.

It seemed only a second that he'd been asleep, but when
Wade next looked for his bed partner, she was gone!

"Sandra?" He bounded out of bed and raced to the
bathroom, expecting to find her there. "Sandy? Sandy!"

Pausing a moment to rake his fingers through his tousled
hair and think, he heard singing coming from somewhere
nearby, followed closely by the welcoming aroma of freshly
brewed coffee.

He raced down the hall and burst into the kitchen as if she
were a burglar he'd caught in the act of robbing him. "What
the hell do you think you're doing?"

Though her eyes raked his bare chest with undisguised
longing, her candid facial expression showed her displea-

sure with both his mood and his language. "Making breakfast."

Wade ran the fingers of both hands through his hair and pushed it back while he struggled to get better control of his emotions. "When I woke up and found you gone I was afraid something had happened to you."

"What could happen to me?" She pulled the old, white, terry robe she had found in the bathroom more tightly around her waist and checked to make sure the sash was secure. "Except maybe running out of clean clothes. I didn't want to come back into the bedroom and wake you, so I put this on. Sorry. I'm afraid it's not very sexy."

That was where she was wrong, Wade thought. Dead wrong. The robe was way too big for her and gaped at the neck whenever she moved. Just seeing her standing there, looking fresh from the shower, wet hair and all, had instantly transported him back to happier days. And nights. Heaven help him if he was close enough to glimpse anything he shouldn't when she bent over in that damn loose bathrobe!

"Anyway, I managed to make the coffee before you woke up." Hesitating, Sandy slipped her hands into the voluminous pockets of the long robe and looked at him quizzically. "I thought I was never going to find the coffeemaker filters, though. Why did you move them?"

"Move them?"

"Uh-huh. They used to be in the cabinet over the stove."

"When?" Wondering if she had finally regained some of her memory, he decided to ask pointed questions and judge for himself. Moments later he was sorry he had.

"Just the other day," Sandy said, shaking her head. "I wish you'd put things back where you find them, that's all. I don't go rearranging your tools in the garage, do I?"

Chagrined, Wade shook his head. "No, I suppose not."

"You're darned right. Now, how about an omelet?"

"I'm not hungry."

"Nonsense. You have to eat before you go to work. I'm certainly well enough to fix you a decent breakfast."

"Which reminds me," Wade said, reaching for the beige telephone mounted on the wall next to the doorway. "I have to call Art and tell him I probably won't be in today."

"Why not?"

"Because you hurt your head," he said with emphasis on each word, as if she were a child.

"I know that. But it's much better this morning. Honest, it is. I hardly even feel the pain." Which was true to a certain extent, she added to herself. Of course, she'd swallowed two more extra-strength aspirin before starting the coffee. Fortunately the medication was beginning to work a little.

"It isn't the knot on your head, Sandra," he said while dialing. "It's all the other stuff."

"*What* other stuff?"

She listened to him speak to his brother, hoping their conversation would shed a bit of light on whatever Wade's problems were, but as far as she could tell, he wasn't making any sense at all.

As soon as he replaced the receiver, she repeated, "What other stuff?" and waited for an answer with her hands planted firmly on her hips.

"Okay," he said, thinking fast. "Look around you. Notice anything new?"

"No, I..." Giving a squeal of delight, she ran to him and threw her arms around his neck. "Oh, honey, I *love* it! You bought me a new fridge!"

Cursing under his breath, he removed her arms and held fast to her wrists to keep her from repeating the affectionate gesture. Why did she have to look so happy, so innocent, so loving all the time?

"No, Sandra," he said firmly. "We—I—have had that refrigerator for over a year. I bought it when the second-hand one we started with gave out."

She shot him an incredulous glance, then grinned up at him. "Oh, sure. And I suppose you expect me to believe I worked around it all that time and didn't notice the change?"

Wade was immediately tempted to fill her in on the harsh reality of their life together. However, he wasn't sure whether that was the approved medical treatment for her present condition and didn't want to chance making things worse. Maybe she had to come out of her amnesia, or whatever it was, by herself.

"I guess I'll have that omelet, after all," he said. "And no onions."

Still grinning broadly, she hurried to admire the new refrigerator while she poked around in it for the carton of eggs. "Got it. No onions."

Her eyes focused on the omelet makings she was looking for, then strayed to the glass shelves and crispers. They looked new, yet they didn't. Not really. Not quite. She paused, thinking about what her husband had claimed and feeling a little as though she'd somehow wandered into the twilight zone.

Straightening with the eggs in one hand, milk and butter balanced in the other and clutched against her chest, she said, "Wade . . . ?"

"Yes?"

"Is that true? About the refrigerator, I mean?"

Now he didn't know what to say. If he pressed for the truth, Sandy's mind might snap. If not, he was apparently stuck with her. Unless . . .

"Don't worry about that right now, okay? Just finish getting our breakfast. I'll be right back. I have another phone call to make."

"Make it in here. You called work from this phone."

"I need to look up a number first. I'll finish getting dressed and catch the phone in the den on my way back."

Sandy watched him turn and leave the kitchen. Beginning to be truly concerned about her apparent aberrations, she folded her arms across her chest, leaned her hip against the counter and gave the entire room a careful perusal. The shiny, brown-and-beige-speckled floor was as she remembered it. So was the oatmeal-colored tile on the countertop, although the grout looked a bit dingy in places.

She blinked hard. The room was literally the same, except for the new refrigerator, of course. If Wade thought it was funny to tease her about losing her memory, he was wrong. It was a lousy joke to play and she intended to tell him so the minute he returned.

Going back into action, she opened the cupboard where she always kept a good-size stack of the canned, green chili peppers she loved to put into her omelets, and peered in. *How strange.*

"What in the...?" Bending lower, she pushed up her sleeve and reached her arm all the way to the rear, clearing away cans of vegetables and fruit as she went but finding none of the little cans of roasted Mexican peppers she was expecting. There wasn't any salsa, either.

Truly puzzled, Sandy straightened. First the coffee filters, now this. Not finding things where she knew they should be was getting on her nerves. So was her husband's bizarre behavior. For a guy who usually loved sex and physical affection he sure was being standoffish.

As a matter of fact, she couldn't remember when they'd last made love. That realization bothered her a lot more than the simple misplacement of a few kitchen items.

Wade looked up the number he wanted and dialed it as soon as he reached the solitude and privacy of his den, tucking in his shirttail and buckling his belt as he listened to the ringing.

It was only a matter of time before Sandy began noticing and questioning other changes he'd made in the house since she'd stopped living there as his wife. When that happened, he wanted another person, preferably a woman, present in case she got hysterical. Although he remembered her relationship with her mother wasn't the best, he didn't know who else to ask.

Violet answered on the fifth ring.

"Mrs. McNamara?"

"Yes. If you're selling something, forget it. I never buy from telephone solicitors."

"It's Wade Walker, Mrs. McNamara. I'm calling about Sandra."

"She never wants to see you again," Violet said loudly and with determination. "Goodbye."

"*Wait!* Don't hang up. Sandra's had a slight accident."

The middle-aged woman made a guttural sound of disgust and disbelief. "Don't be silly. Why would you know about something like that? If there was a problem with my daughter, I'm sure she would have contacted me, not you."

"That was what I thought," Wade said. "Only she showed up here yesterday afternoon acting like she thought we were still married."

"Oh, my God! What have you done to her?"

"Nothing."

"You expect me to believe that? Put Sandra on the line. I want to speak with her myself."

"Uh, I can't right now. She doesn't know I'm calling you. I thought it would be best if you just came over and saw for yourself what the problem is. That way, if she does wind up needing medical treatment, you can go with her."

"Medical treatment? How badly is she hurt?"

About time you got around to asking, Wade thought. "She got a bump on her head. Apparently, it's left her pretty confused."

"I'll say, if she came to you for help."

He purposely ignored the insult. "How soon can you get here?"

"Why don't you bring her to me, instead? You know I don't like to drive."

"Because she's not acting like herself. I'm not sure how far I can push her without doing more harm than good."

"Ha! Since when were you concerned about that?"

"Look," Wade said, choosing his words carefully. "I don't care what you think of me. The important consideration right now is your daughter. Are you coming or not?"

"I'll have to call a cab," Violet said. "An idiotic judge took my driver's license away a few months ago."

Drinking and driving, Wade thought, glad the authorities had finally cracked down on his ex-mother-in-law. "Fine. You do that. I'll keep her as happy and calmed down as I can till you get here."

"Don't do her any favors," the woman snapped. "Just make sure that you keep your hands off her or I'll see you in court. Is that clear?"

"Perfectly," Wade said coldly. He hung up the receiver wondering how such a shrew had turned out a daughter like the Sandy McNamara he had met and married.

Reminiscing, he recalled the other side of his supposedly flawless bride's personality, the side that had surfaced to cost him so dearly.

Viewing the situation in that harsh manner helped in a way, he decided as he made his way to the bathroom to shave before breakfast.

He must remember the tragic events that led up to their divorce at all costs, Wade told himself. Even if it was the hardest thing he'd ever called upon himself to do.

Sandy was singing again when he returned to the kitchen. Her cooking smelled heavenly, although she had left one of her legendary messes all over the sink and stove.

Wade couldn't help but smile at the sight. Some things never changed, did they?

"Oh, good. You're just in time to sit down and keep me company," she said with a come-hither glance.

"Only if the invitation includes whatever you've cooked."

"Fine thing. And I thought you married me for my body."

I did, partly, he admitted ruefully as he seated himself at the maple dining table in the corner. "Nope. It was your fantastic cooking that got to me."

"That's good to know," Sandy quipped. "At least there was one thing you liked about me that I can still do pretty well." She carried two filled plates to the table and joined him. "Eat. I want you to keep your strength up."

Raising an eyebrow, Wade glanced over at her. "Why?"

"For when I'm all better. By my recollection, you and I are at least a week behind in the lovemaking department."

He choked on the bite of food he'd popped into his mouth while she was talking. Coughing, he bent over as Sandy slapped him on the back.

"Whoa," she said with a giggle. "I didn't think my subtle little reminder was going to prove fatal!"

Subtle? "I'm fine." Wade cleared his throat by drinking from the large glass of orange juice she'd set beside his coffee cup on the table. "Just swallowed wrong, that's all."

"Good. Then maybe you'll explain to me why you've been treating me as if I had the plague or something." She placed her hand gently on his forearm and felt the muscles beneath her fingers tense. "Please tell me what's bothering you. I'm sure we can fix it if we talk it over."

The way we did before? Wade grimaced. "Let's just concentrate on finishing this great meal, shall we? Then we'll clean up the kitchen together."

"Oh, leave it," Sandy urged. "Since you're not going to work and I have this awful headache, I think we should just kick back and relax today."

Concerned again, he studied her. "You said your head was better. Is it or isn't it?"

"It is. It is. Honest. I just hate to do dishes. You know that."

"Yes, but your mother's coming over this morning. You don't want her to see the mess you left, do you?"

Sandy made a pouting, purposely absurd comic face to show her displeasure without actually voicing it. "She is? Wonderful. How did that happen?"

"It's a long story."

"I'll bet it is. I hope she's sober for once."

"Me, too. I guess I should have asked if your dad was available to come with her."

Sandy's brow knit. "You talked to her? When?"

"This morning," he said, deciding to fill her in on part of the conversation so she'd know Violet's upcoming visit wasn't totally off-the-wall. "That was who I called when I went to use the phone in the den."

"Boy, you *are* mad at me, aren't you?"

Touched by the little-girl-lost expression on her face, Wade reached out and covered her hand with his. "Actually, Sandy," he said with total honesty, "I'm probably less mad at you at this moment than I have been for a very long time."

She brightened, her smile so genuine and so appealing he thought his heart would burst with the beauty of it.

"Good," she said, responding to the love and desire she saw in his darkly passionate gaze. "Then kiss me."

To his infinite amazement, Wade leaned over and did exactly that.

Warm and sweet, her lips softened beneath his, touching him more profoundly than he'd thought possible. There was nothing overtly sexual in the light, tender kiss, yet it took his breath away.

Feeling himself beginning to tremble inside he quickly broke the contact and stepped back. "Come on," he said, clearing his throat to give himself a few more seconds to recover. "I'll help you with the dishes."

"I'd rather stay right here and kiss you," she purred.

Wade rolled his eyes. Taking her by the shoulders he literally turned her around to face the cluttered sink. "We'll discuss that later. Right now, we both have work to do."

"Killjoy."

Making a guttural sound of disgust and nodding his head, Wade said, "Lady, you have *no* idea."

Chapter Four

Seated at the kitchen table, enjoying a last cup of coffee, both Wade and Sandy were startled by Violet McNamara's noisy arrival and imminent intrusion on their temporary domestic peace. Hearing the front door slam, they shot each other silent looks of empathy across the table.

Dressed in a flowing, silk caftan whose colors echoed her name, Violet burst into the kitchen, her dyed, reddish hair a wildly fluffy halo of curls around her thin face.

"*There* you are," she shouted, wagging a well-manicured index finger in the air and directing her considerable ire toward Wade, while virtually ignoring her daughter. "How *dare* you take advantage of this poor girl!"

Leaning back, he merely shrugged off the unjust accusation. "I suggest you remember who called and asked you to come here this morning."

Sandy made a face at him as she entered the heated conversation. "I'm still trying to figure out why he did that, Mother," she said, spreading her hands wide in a gesture of abeyance. "As you can see, I'm perfectly fine. I fell off my bicycle yesterday, but..."

"He pushed you?" Violet offered. "Is that what happened?"

"No, of course not." Sandy was shaking her head slowly, pensively, and staring at the coffee remaining in her cup. "He wasn't even there. I was riding alone."

"Naturally you were," her mother said in a huff. "Why on earth would you be with this...*man?*"

"Because he's my husband," Sandy said, evidently confused about the unusually strong vehemence with which her mother was attacking Wade.

Violet threw her hands into the air, her caftan sleeves billowing, and began pacing while she wailed a refined version of curses. "I thought we were through with this nonsense!"

"Mother, for heaven's sake," Sandy said with forced calm. "Pull yourself together. Remember what Dr. Schwartz said."

"Doctor who?" Violet's lavender eye shadow crinkled into little creases as she squinted over at the younger woman.

"Dr. Schwartz. I know how much you and Dad value his professional advice. I distinctly recall him telling you to slow down and try to approach things in a rational manner, especially if you'd been..."

"Drinking? Is that what you're getting at? Well, forget it. All I've had this morning are a couple of Bloody Marys and some buttered toast. Besides, that particular doctor retired years ago. What makes you bring him up now?"

Sandy cast a puzzled glance at Wade. "He did? I don't seem to remember that, do you?"

Stretching out her long, tapering fingers, Violet grabbed the sleeve of the white robe and tugged on her daughter's arm. "What do you mean, you don't remember?"

"I—I just don't." Sandy combed the fingers of her free hand through her still-damp hair to lift it back from her forehead.

Violet tightened her grasp. "What else don't you remember?"

That ridiculous question made Sandy giggle in spite of her mother's clearly hostile attitude. "If I don't remember, how would I know what I've forgotten?"

"Well, let me tell you something, missy..."

Wade interrupted by getting to his feet and purposefully encircling his former mother-in-law's wrist with his large, strong hand. Violet stiffened and recoiled as he'd hoped she would and he spoke directly to her, easily holding her light-weight frame immobile. "I don't think it's a good idea to force any more unnecessary information on Sandra while she's still so confused, Mrs. McNamara."

She jerked her arm free, her myriad bracelets jangling like Gypsy jewelry in a Halloween ensemble. "Of course you don't. You don't fool me, Wade Walker. The longer she stays bewildered like this, the better chance you have of taking worse advantage of her."

"Mother!" Sandy went swiftly to Wade's side and stepped into the shelter of his arms. "How can you think such awful things, let alone say them? I've told you before, Wade is my husband and I love him."

"Oh, dear Lord. He's hypnotized you!"

Smiling up at him with clear affection, Sandy agreed. "You bet he has. And I've loved every minute of it, too."

"That does it," Violet said, reaching for the telephone on the wall. "I'm calling the police."

Wade's hand over the receiver effectively stopped the action as he glared down at her. "And what do you plan to tell them?"

"That my daughter is not in her right mind!"

"What will that accomplish? Sandra needs medical care, not a trip to a psychiatric ward." He stepped past Violet and started toward the back of the house, his unresisting former wife in tow, her mother following closely. "As soon as she's dressed, I'm taking her to the urgent-care clinic. I talked to a doctor there last night, and I'm going to see that she gets a thorough physical examination."

"Nonsense. She's my daughter and she's coming with me."

"Stop it! Both of you," Sandy insisted loudly. She pulled away to stand by herself in the doorway to the master suite. "I agree I may need to see a doctor, but I assure you, I *don't* need to be treated like a child."

Wade backed off just far enough to allow Sandy the freedom she seemed to want without giving Violet an easy opportunity to wedge herself between them. He realized he'd been wrong to bring the other woman into the current situation. If he had recalled just how unstable Violet McNamara was, he wouldn't have made the call to her on Sandra's behalf in the first place. Now it was up to him to remove that troublesome obstacle.

Smiling reassuringly at Sandy, he said, "Okay. Sorry, honey. Go get some clothes on and I'll drive you to the clinic."

Violet snorted in derision. "That won't be necessary. I have a cab waiting."

"Good." Sandy gazed at her mother with firm though tender resolve. "That means Wade and I won't have to take you home first. I promise I'll call and tell you what the doctor says so you don't worry."

"Worry? I never worry. I simply take matters into my own hands and solve my problems for myself, as you should," the older woman said flatly. "That's why I'm the one who's going to take you to see the doctor."

Sandy sighed and cast a telling look at Wade. "See what you can do to pacify her, will you," she whispered as she pivoted to enter the bedroom. "I'll get dressed as fast as I can and come back to rescue you."

Closing the door behind her, she stood in the quiet for a moment to listen for whatever bits of conversation filtered through the walls. Thankfully, all seemed peaceful for the moment. If her mother's alcohol-laced breakfast got the better of her, though, Sandy knew she might be forced to intervene, and that was honestly the last thing she wanted to have to do, given her own current problems.

Not that reasoning with Violet had ever been easy, Sandy reminded herself. As a child, she had often tried to play peacemaker between her warring parents. Whether or not her efforts were successful depended mostly upon how much her mother had had to drink that day and what kind of a mood her harried father was in. Most of the time, he was either leaving or arriving home for one of his short stays, so none of their arguments lasted long anyway.

Pensive, Sandy walked slowly across the soft carpet. What a shame her parents had never found the love and acceptance she had in her marriage. If she hadn't experienced it for herself with Wade, she might never have believed such peace and happiness were possible.

She smiled. *Lord, I love that man,* she thought, nearly overcome by the realization that no matter what happened, he would always be there for her. And she for him, she added with a widening grin, a few happy tears momentarily clouding her vision. She might not be the luckiest woman in the world, but she was certainly in the forefront.

Going to the dresser, Sandy opened the top drawer, then paused, puzzled, before rummaging through the socks and underwear inside. How odd. Wade must have done the laundry while she was in the mountains and absentmindedly put his personal things in the drawer she always reserved for herself.

Shrugging, she opened the next drawer, then the next and the next, till all six had been thoroughly searched. A shiver ran up her spine to tickle the hair on the back of her neck. What was going on here? Where were all her clothes?

Leaving the dresser as it stood, she hurried to the closet and slid open the double doors. Her mouth dropped open, her eyes widening. The shirts, slacks and suits hanging there obviously belonged to Wade, yet there was no sign of anything feminine. Nothing. Not even a single pair of shoes.

She spotted her tennis shoes lying by the side of the bed where Wade had dropped them when he'd removed them the night before. Suddenly they seemed like the only real objects in the room. Gathering them up, Sandy hugged them to her chest, oblivious to the dust and the occasional pine needle falling to the floor at her feet.

"I am here, where I belong," she told herself. "This is my house and my husband."

Waiting for her memory to contradict her, she found no such reaction forthcoming. Therefore, she reasoned, there had to be a logical explanation for the seeming inconsistencies between what she felt was right and what present experience seemed to be telling her.

Before she was conscious of the movement, Sandy was hurrying toward the bedroom door, toward the man in whom she placed her complete trust. To her enormous relief, he was standing just outside like a sentinel.

He glanced over his shoulder when he heard her opening the door. "What is it?" He scanned her slight form, noting that she still wore the terry robe and was now clutching her shoes to her chest, causing the lapels of the robe to gape just enough above the tops of her softly rounded breasts to momentarily steal his breath away.

He recovered to ask, "What's wrong?"

"My... my clothes," Sandy said, sounding distraught. "Where are they, Wade?"

"In the guest bathroom, I guess, from when you took a shower. Want me to get them for you?"

Sandy stood on tiptoe and began whispering. "No. I mean all my clean clothes."

Cursing, he spun around, ducked into the bedroom and slammed the door behind him in spite of Violet's loud protests. Grabbing clothing from the open drawers and the closet, he threw the garments in a heap on the bed. "Put those on for now and hurry up, okay? Your mother is threatening to tear me apart."

"But..."

He had returned to the door, opened it, and was effectively blocking the older woman's view of the scene with his broad shoulders. "Just do it. I'll be right out here, waiting."

Watching him leave and slam the door tight behind him, Sandy felt so bereft she almost broke down and wept. Wade knew she was still sore all over from the fall she'd taken. The least he could have done was offer to help her get dressed, even if he didn't want to bother to produce the particular clothes she'd asked for.

She began to dress slowly, cautiously, trying to keep from aggravating her bruised knees and skinned elbow. The blue-striped sport shirt and nylon shorts Wade had tossed onto the bed were way too big for her, but she guessed it was better than going outside in the robe or, worse, having to don her dirty clothes from the bicycle wreck.

Buttoning the top three buttons of the shirt, she tied its long tail in a knot at the front of her waist above the elastic band of the shorts to help hide the fact she was braless, slipped into her shoes and headed for the door.

She wouldn't make a scene with her mother present, but Wade had better get ready to explain what was really going on as soon as they were alone again. Something was definitely not right in their cozy little world and no way was it all because she'd fallen and gotten a simple lump on her head.

No, sir. More than that was affecting them and somebody had better volunteer to explain pretty soon or she was going to insist on it. After all, this was her house, her husband and her life. Nothing was ever going to change that as long as she had anything to say about it.

"My God, Sandra!" Violet exclaimed the moment the young woman emerged from the bedroom. "Where did you get those awful clothes?"

Sandy smiled at her mother's predictable snobbishness, then struck a pose. "They're the latest from Seventh Avenue, Mom. I thought for sure you'd have heard about the new casual trend from New York designers by now."

"I most certainly have not!"

"Too bad." Sandy took Wade's arm and started for the front door. "Well, we have to be going. See you later."

"Listen," Violet insisted, hot on their trail, "I did not raise my only daughter to run around dressed like a refugee from the rag bag. You can't go anywhere looking like that! What will my friends say?"

Wade glanced back at her. "Maybe nobody important will see us," he said sarcastically. "Besides, that shirt is practically new."

"I didn't think I remembered it," Sandy said, gazing up at him. "It's a nice color. Bet it looks fabulous on you with your tan." She ran her palm lightly over the sharp planes of his cheek in a swift caress.

His jaw clenched. "Thanks."

"You're quite welcome." This felt more normal, Sandy thought, clinging to Wade's arm as they made their way out to the driveway. Parked there was the station wagon containing her wrecked bike, and the taxi her mother had mentioned.

Wade reached into his pocket and pushed the button on a remote control to open the garage door on the opposite side of the double drive. As it slid up, Sandy noticed a shiny, black pickup truck in the place where she had expected to see the classic Mustang he always drove.

She halted, grasping his arm. "What happened to Matilda?"

His first inclination was to remind her she had wrecked the old car in the midst of the turmoil surrounding their original breakup, but he immediately thought better of it. Instead he reassured her. "Matilda the Mustang is retired for the present," Wade said calmly. "I needed a truck in my business and it made a dandy tax deduction, so I bought myself one of those new Dodge Rams with the Cummins diesel engine."

"It's beautiful," Sandy said, approaching the garage beside him. "But so big!"

He opened the passenger door for her. "I added running boards so it would be easy to get in and out. Think you can make it okay?"

"Sure."

Violet had not given up. "I'm still here, Sandra," she called from beside the taxi. "You don't have to go with that man, you know. You do have a choice."

"Thanks, but no, thanks, Mother," Sandy shouted back as she climbed stiffly aboard. "I'll be fine."

Wade circled the truck and got in. "You will, you know," he said, reaching over to help her adjust her safety belt. He started the powerful engine. "I promise I'll get you whatever help you need."

"Just being near you and knowing that you care is probably all I need to get well," she said with a contented smile. "You have no idea how glad I am to be home. I don't know why, but sometimes I get the feeling I've been gone forever."

Wade's hands tightened on the wheel as he steered into the street, shifted gears and pressed the accelerator hard. "Yeah," he said, gritting his teeth. "I know just what you mean."

They were several blocks from the house when Sandy remembered she hadn't brought along her purse and mentioned the omission to Wade. "We really should go back for it."

"It won't be necessary," he argued. "I can take care of everything for you."

"I know you can." She paused, thinking. "It's just that I feel . . . I don't know . . . like I should have it with me. I suppose it's silly to worry about such a simple thing."

He glanced over at her. Her concern had wrinkled her brow and cast a shadow over her countenance. There was no hurry getting to the doctor, he reasoned, yet if he agreed to return to the house for her handbag, there was every chance Sandy would look inside it and discover just how seriously disoriented she was. How dangerous would that be? he wondered.

Sandy reached over and touched his arm. "Wade?"

"What?"

"I want to go back home."

"I told you, I can take care of everything. If they insist on immediate payment I'll just write a check. You don't need your purse."

Tears were filling her eyes and threatening to spill out over her dark lashes. "It's not that. Not exactly. I just have this really uneasy feeling that I have to have my purse. I can't help it if I'm not making any sense. Please?"

One quick look told him it would be best to comply with her wishes, at least temporarily. Signaling for a turn, he rounded the corner and headed back toward his house, grateful to see her relaxing almost immediately.

"Thanks," she said.

"You're welcome."

He turned a second corner, then a third, and pulled to a stop in the street in front of the modest, ranch-style house he'd bought as an investment several years before he and Sandy had decided to marry and live there.

The house had been on the market for six months right after their divorce, but he'd priced it so high there was little chance of it selling. In his heart, he knew that. He also knew that living there, alone, brought back painful memories. The trouble was, he'd gotten so used to having those memories for company he found he missed them too much to seriously consider letting them go by actually selling the house.

"You wait here," Wade ordered as he got out of the pickup. "I'll get your purse and be right back."

Sandy released her safety belt. "I can do it."

"No." His voice was purposely forceful.

The no-nonsense tone caused her to pause and settle back into the seat. She watched him jog effortlessly across the lawn and up the steps to the broad, cement porch. He was so sweet, so good to her. A satisfied, happy smile lifted the corners of her mouth and she laid her head back against the soft upholstery and closed her eyes, the warm sun caressing her face and making her drowsy.

Life was so wonderful. So perfect. She had her husband, her home, a job she loved— Sandy's eyes popped open. Work! In the confusion surrounding her injury, she'd forgotten all about her job at the school. What would they think when she didn't show up and hadn't even called in sick? Starting to get out of the truck to go into the house to phone the elementary school, she hesitated when she saw Wade returning. He had her beige shoulder bag tucked under his arm.

"I have to make a call," she said as soon as he was close enough to hear.

"Why?"

"If I don't, Mrs. Lynch will think I've deserted her."

"Mrs. who?"

"The teacher I work for. You remember, don't you? My instructional-aide job?"

Wade remembered, all right. Sandy hadn't worked for the school for at least three years that he knew of. She'd quit to concentrate fully on her college education before they were even married.

"You can call from a pay phone at the clinic," he said, starting the truck again and pulling away from the curb before she had a chance to argue.

She refastened her seat belt and looked at him quizzically. "What time is it anyway?"

"A little after ten."

Sandy sighed. "First recess. Oh, well, I'm good and late already. I guess a few more minutes won't matter one way or the other."

She pulled her purse onto her lap, unzipped the top and began to rummage around. Everything seemed perfectly normal. The contents were characteristically messy, but that was the way a woman's bag was supposed to be, wasn't it, so why had she felt such a strong urge to have it with her?

Lifting out her red leather wallet, she flipped it open, expecting to see her driver's license and photo. Instead, there was an empty spot in the ID pocket. The plastic folder with her family pictures was gone, too.

Sandy tensed. "Wade?"

"Uh-huh."

"Something's wrong."

He glanced over at her with a puzzled expression. "What?"

"My license and the photos I always kept in here are missing."

"Nonsense. You probably just mislaid them."

She poked around in the clutter some more. "No, I don't think so." Looking further, she was relieved to find the few credit cards she normally used and held them up for him to see. "At least I still have these. That's good news."

Wade's hands tightened on the wheel. He'd overlooked the cards, although it seemed no harm was done. Besides, any greater delay might have made Sandra suspect him of tampering with her purse and he couldn't allow that.

Once the doctors at the clinic had examined her and assured him it would do no harm to let her know precisely how out of touch with reality she was, he'd return the missing items and see her safely home and out of his life. Until then, the license and photos were hidden in his pocket.

He chanced a quick, sidelong glance. Hugging the soft leather purse to her body like a teddy bear, Sandy was staring straight ahead, her lips pressed into a tight line, her chin jutting out stubbornly. It wasn't going to be easy to convince her she was hallucinating, no matter how many medical men agreed or insisted. Until now, she had always been strong-willed and sure of herself, no matter what. He guessed that came from her harsh upbringing and the fact that she'd been more of a parent than a child for most of her young life, taking care of her mother and father as if she alone understood their problems.

He'd thought they could work through her hang-ups together and eventually make a life for themselves as husband and wife, but he'd been wrong. Dead wrong. Sandy didn't understand the meaning of being a family. Some scars went too deep for even love to heal.

Blinking to clear his vision, he concentrated on the road and his driving, trying to subvert his emotions and insulate himself from the feelings he couldn't help having for the young woman seated next to him.

He had just about succeeded, too, when she looked over at him with those big, misty, hazel eyes of hers and said, "Wade, I'm scared. I'm really scared."

Chapter Five

The Emergency Medical Clinic on Tyler Avenue was bustling with activity when Sandy entered with Wade at her side. He explained having telephoned the day before, requested to have Sandy see Dr. Simmondson, then sat with her and helped her try to fill out the new-patient forms till her name was finally called.

Sandy handed the clipboard with the information sheets on it to the businesslike, blond nurse, who weighed her and then took her to an examining room.

"I'm afraid I don't remember some things too well," Sandy explained. "I fell off my bike and hit my head."

"That's what your husband told us," the nurse said, beginning to write on a new file folder and sort out the forms Sandy had been working on. "I see here that you list your age as twenty-three. Is that correct?"

"Yes."

"And you're certain about the year of your birth?"

"Of course I am." She held still while the other woman took her pulse, temperature and blood pressure.

"Did you vote for the current president of the United States?"

"I...I think so," Sandy said, wondering why a complete stranger wanted to know her political leanings.

"And who would that be?"

Panic filled Sandy's mind. She could envision the president's face, but that was all the information she could muster, and her deficiency of memory was frightening. Instinctively she tried to cover the shortcoming. "Um, I remember he's a tall man."

"I see." The nurse made more notes in her file, then straightened and put her stethoscope into the pocket of her crisp, white smock. "You just make yourself comfortable, Mrs. Walker, and the doctor will be in to see you in a few minutes, as soon as he gets done stitching up the Osgood boy."

Sandy brightened. Now, *there* was something she could relate to. "Bobby Osgood? A little guy about eight years old? I know him from my teacher's-aide job at the school. He's a real terror. Would you like me to help you control his bad behavior? I assure you, I'm very good at things like that."

"Thank you. I'm sure you are. But it won't be necessary. This boy is much older, so he can't be the one you know," the nurse said with a nod and a brief smile. "Have a seat, please. It won't be long. And I'll look in on you from time to time if the doctor gets delayed, okay?"

"Okay." Left alone in the stuffy, closed room, Sandy looked around for something, anything, to take her mind off her pounding headache and the confusion she was feeling about nearly everything. It wasn't that she doubted the accuracy of her clear memories. It was all the other stuff, such as who the current president was. Darned if she knew, and she made it a point to vote in every election because she so highly valued her freedom to help choose the country's leaders.

A rack of dog-eared magazines mounted against the pale, greenish wall caught her eye. Clearly used, they looked as if they'd been there for years. Still, reading something to take her mind off her troubles had to be better than sitting there worrying.

She recognized the cover design of the magazine in the front of the rack, picked the magazine up and checked the date, immediately pleased. It was more than current! It must be an early release, she reasoned, because it was a holiday issue and the fall of the year was still many months away.

It was, however, the correct year, and that knowledge gave Sandy an immense sense of relief. She began to slowly turn the pages, wondering vaguely how such a recent publication had gotten so tattered in the short time it had been available. Choosing to read an article on making Thanksgiving table decorations, she was halfway through when the doctor rapped on the door, let himself in and began to talk to her.

"Well, you were right," Simmondson told Wade in the privacy of his office. "That lady is really out of it." He cracked a smile. "She even remarked on how current our magazines were, and I can't remember the last time we got any new ones."

"I noticed. The one I leafed through while I was waiting still had the Rams playing in L.A."

"Yeah." The slim, balding doctor rested himself on the edge of his desk, laced his fingers together and shook his head. "We don't have the fancy equipment to do a complete workup on your wife, but I did order a skull series taken and the X rays show there's no serious cranial damage."

"Then what's wrong with her?" Wade had spent one of the longest mornings of his life waiting for word of Sandy's condition and he wasn't feeling very patient at the moment.

"I would say she's suffering from temporary disorienting trauma."

"Which means?" Wade's voice was anything but calm.

"In laymen's terms, it resembles the antiquated, broad-
spectrum diagnosis of amnesia," Simmondson said. "She
won't know much about current events, such as who's in
office in Washington, but she's in no immediate danger."

"You're sure about that?"

"I'm sure." He withdrew a pad of paper from his pocket
and began to scrawl on it. "I'll prescribe something to help
with her headache. I've already instructed her to make an
appointment with her personal physician if she's not better
in a week or so. I trust you'll see that she follows through."

"Of course."

The doctor looked Wade straight in the eye and added,
"She'll also need someone to keep tabs on her in case she
has any other delusions."

"Is that likely?"

"It could be. In cases like this, there's no way to tell. The
important thing is to make sure she stays out of trouble till
she returns to normal. Does she have family nearby?"

"Only an alcoholic mother and an absent father."

"And you."

Wade threw up his hands in a gesture of denial. "Oh, no.
Not me. She and I parted company years ago."

"But you still care about her," the doctor observed with
a wry smile.

"Who says?"

"You do. You took her in last night and brought her for
treatment this morning. I don't see that as the act of a man
who has given up caring."

"I couldn't just throw her out into the street, could I? I
mean, she was so hurt and lost, like a child."

Simmondson smiled again. "That wife of yours is no kid,
Mr. Walker. As a matter of fact, she's quite a lovely woman.
Maybe you should reconsider and let her stay with you, at

least until you can locate a friend or relative who will agree to take over.''

''For how long?''

''A week. Maybe two. I doubt the condition will last longer than that. As soon as the swelling starts to go down you should begin to see improvement in her memory and orientation.''

''Meaning, I could be stuck with her for goodness knows how long.''

''Worse things could happen.''

''That,'' Wade said, starting for the office door, ''has to be the understatement of the year.''

Sandy was waiting for him, her purse clutched to her chest, when Wade returned. ''Well,'' she asked, her voice quavering slightly, ''will I live?''

''Long and happily,'' he said, taking her arm and heading for the door. ''You should be back to normal in no time.''

She breathed a sigh of relief. ''Wow. That's good news.'' Smiling, she looked up at him. ''I can tell you who the president is.''

Wade paused expectantly. Maybe he'd be through with his unofficial job as Sandy's rescuer sooner than the doctor had thought. ''You can?''

''Uh-huh. I read it in the *Time* magazine in the waiting room.'' She stood on tiptoe to whisper the name in his ear.

Clearing his throat to hide his disappointment with the outdated news, Wade nodded. ''Good for you. Now, how about some lunch? I'm starved.''

''Okay. Let's get a pizza or something and take it home, though. This morning has been a real ordeal and I could use some peace and quiet.''

Agreeing, he helped her into the pickup and then circled around to join her. By the time he slid behind the wheel, she had lifted the center console and scooted over to sit imme-

diately next to him. Her innocence and complete trust
caused a lump to form in his throat.

He cocked his head toward the passenger side of the
truck's enormous cab. "You'd better go back over there and
put on your seat belt. You know the law."

"I do?" Sandy made a face. "Actually, I have no idea
what you're talking about, but that doesn't matter." She
began to grin at him. "I found another belt right here in the
middle."

Wade clenched his teeth. Damn efficient engineers. He
knew he'd bought a state-of-the-art vehicle. At the moment, however, he was wishing its designers hadn't been
quite so competent. His wishes quadrupled when Sandy
snuggled closer and laid her hand on his thigh, massaging
it the way she always used to.

"You shouldn't do that," he warned.

The slim hand slid higher, the fingers probing more inti-
mately.

"Really? Since when?"

Wanting to respond in kind, but knowing he would be
taking terrible advantage of Sandy's disorientation, Wade
seriously considered getting out of the truck and running
around the parking lot to try to regain some of his deterio-
rating self-control.

Instead he grasped her roving hand and held it tightly for
a moment, then gave in to his deepest desires and brought
it to his lips, gently kissing the smooth fingertips that had
once given him so much intimate pleasure.

"I can't concentrate on my driving if you touch me like
that," he said honestly. Her eyes had taken on a dreamy
quality, and when she looked up at him and said, "Good,"
he thought for an instant of actually grabbing her and
making passionate love to her right there on the seat of the
truck.

He was breathing hard when he released her, and purposely stared straight ahead, placing his hands firmly on the

steering wheel. "Sandra, stop taunting me. Give it up. I'm not going to weaken and do something we'll both be sorry for, no matter how much you tease."

"Okay," she said.

She was exhibiting the sly, all-knowing look he'd seen her use most often when they were in bed together, and Wade stiffened. What had he gotten himself into? This was no stray puppy he was befriending—this was Sandy. His Sandy. The more freedom he denied her, the more she would demand, he knew. It was simply her nature.

Pensive, Sandy relaxed and slid her hand through the crook of Wade's arm as she laid her head on his shoulder. It *was* okay—or at least, it would be, she reasoned. Clearly her husband was worried about her injury, and it was just like him to coddle her, even though she knew she didn't need to be treated like some fragile flower. So, she'd humor him, even though his negative attitude was hurting her feelings. After all, he had just as much right to postpone having sex, for whatever reasons, as she did.

So much for modern-day equality, she thought with a sigh. Not that she would want to regress and see any woman live under the trying circumstances she'd watched her mother struggle to bear. Maybe there was a reason, however tenuous, for Violet to have taken refuge in alcohol after all.

Sandy tightened her grip on Wade's arm and felt his muscles flex. "Okay, I'll be good," she said with a further squeeze. "Just take me home."

He started the engine. "First we'll stop and pick up lunch, as you wanted. How about Marino's?"

"Oh, that's perfect. I love their food." She closed her eyes and gave herself over to complete reliance on her husband. After all, he was the only stable and predictable person in her life right now. Without him as an anchor and a safe haven, she didn't know what she'd do.

Wade wondered if his companion was actually sleeping or simply resting. Judging by her relaxed hold on his arm, he suspected the former. Pulling into the parking lot at the familiar Italian restaurant, he gently nudged her. "Sandy? We're here."

"Um?" She opened her eyes and smiled up at him. "I guess I must have dozed off."

"I'm not sure. You didn't snore," Wade quipped.

She elbowed him in the ribs and stretched. "I never snore. Ladies don't do such things."

With that, he laughed and opened his door to climb out. "Right. Come on."

"But..." Sandy was peering out the windshield. "I thought you said we were going to Marino's?"

"We are. This is Marino's."

"It can't be." Moving slowly, as if in a dream state, she unfastened her safety belt, slid the rest of the way to his side of the truck because it was closer and stepped down onto the pavement beside him. "Marino's is a little hole-in-the-wall place that makes great pizza. It's a mom-and-pop business. This is a real restaurant."

Wade hadn't thought about when the changes in their favorite eatery had taken place. Apparently Sandy's memories were crystal clear about an earlier, simpler time. He stayed close to her side while she approached the front door of the establishment as if sneaking up on a sleeping tiger. When she turned to gaze up at him, there was apprehension and doubt in her eyes.

"I—I honestly don't remember any of this."

"It'll be all right," he assured her, placing his hand protectively at the small of her back and escorting her inside. "You will."

"When?"

"Soon. The doctor says it won't be long at all till you're back to normal."

She gazed up at him and tried to smile. "I sure hope I recognize what's normal when I see it. Thank goodness I have you to turn to for moral support."

Wade steeled himself for the moment when her aberrations would finally cease and she would realize just how much she had compromised herself in that regard. He had no doubt that before long she would recall their rocky past and regress to the impossibly difficult person she had become as a result of their ultimate breakup.

Therefore his real concern had to be the present, the memories they were creating by being together under one roof, ostensibly as husband and wife. When Sandy did finally recover her memory, he hoped to hell she also retained the knowledge that he hadn't laid a hand on her, so to speak. If not, there was likely to be more no-holds-barred confrontation than the last time they had separated for keeps.

Sandy managed to keep calm by convincing herself the restaurant was new and had nothing to do with the comfortable, casual place she recollected. Thankfully Wade did not try to dissuade her from ordering their meal to take home. If he had offered any argument, she was ready to insist that she was not properly dressed to lunch in such an elegant setting.

There was a real, three-tiered fountain in the foyer, she noted, and live green plants everywhere, giving the illusion that the patrons were dining in a garden. Red linen cloths covered the tables. In the diffuse light, Sandy could see that the waiters were costumed to coordinate with the decor and the Italian setting. All in all, it was a charming place, even though she swore she'd never been there before.

Perusing the menu, she sat beside Wade on a burgundy, leather-covered bench near the fountain. "I'll have the lasagna and a spinach salad."

"Doesn't surprise me," he said. "You love the way they make it here."

"I do? Good, because my stomach is beginning to agree with you that it's time to eat."

Leaving her, he ordered from the hostess, paid for their meal, then returned to the bench to wait. He was trying to think of something casual and noncommittal to say, when he spied an old acquaintance exiting the dining room with a lovely young woman on his arm.

Robert Sullivan. Chamber of commerce past president and a customer of his from the print shop. And with a woman other than the usually taciturn Mrs. Sullivan! Wade's heart leaped to his throat. Of all the rotten luck! The last thing poor Sandra needed was someone else from their past to come along and confuse her more than she already was.

Clearly the other man recognized them both, because he approached with his right hand outstretched. "Wade, you old son of a gun! And Sandy. Never thought I'd see the day."

Wade stood to greet him and hopefully put a damper on the volatile situation before it got out of hand. "Hello, Robert."

Cautious, Sandra held back. This person seemed to know her, but although his booming voice sounded vaguely familiar, she had absolutely no idea who he might be. Of course, meeting and talking to him might jog her memory, she reasoned, getting to her feet to stand beside Wade.

The men were still shaking hands and she didn't like the way either of them was eyeing her. Wade was acting ashamed of her and the other man was leering as if she were the main attraction in a cheap girlie show.

Nevertheless she extended her hand to him. "Good to see you."

He seemed taken aback. "Yeah, sure. I don't think either of you know Melissa."

They exchanged pleasant greetings, then everyone fell silent. It was clear to Sandy that Wade wished he were anywhere but there. After what seemed like an eternity, he mumbled an excuse, took the other man by the arm and ushered him outside. When Sandy started to follow, he ordered her to wait where she was.

Melissa, also abandoned, joined her on the bench. "I suppose you think I'm terrible, huh?"

"I beg your pardon?"

"For dating a married man." She puckered her precisely defined brows beneath a frill of pale-blond bangs and batted her long lashes. "Since you and your husband obviously know my Robbie from before, I figured you'd hold it against me."

"Not at all," Sandy said, her mind casting about for a follow-up question that wouldn't sound too odd. "You and I have never met, right?"

The young woman looked at her and blinked. "No, not that I know of. Rob and his wife have been separated for a long time, so I guess he might have dated other girls before he started seeing me. Maybe you're thinking of one of them."

"Probably." On the periphery of her vision, Sandy could see the men engaged in a heated discussion on the sidewalk outside. Every few seconds, one or the other of them would glance back at her, then off they'd go again, talking and gesturing.

Where she wanted to be was in the midst of the fray, listening to whatever they were debating. She was positive it related to her, whether Wade was revealing her recent trauma or not, and she knew that if she was present there was a fair chance the conversation would stimulate her wounded memory. Getting to her feet, she excused herself from Melissa and walked purposely for the door.

Wade saw her coming. Whirling, he headed her off, took her in his arms in an openly protective embrace and led her as far from the other people as the rather confining space would allow. All Sandy saw of his old friend was the man's rapid departure with his paramour.

"Why were you two arguing?"

"Who says we were?" Wade asked.

"I do. It looked like you were about to come to blows. And who was Melissa? She says she's dating your friend but he's still married to someone else."

"Barbara. They got married a few years before we did."

"Barbara? The name sounds familiar." Sandy rubbed her temples. "Maybe if my head didn't hurt so much I could remember her."

Wade cursed under his breath. "The doctor gave me a prescription for you, and I didn't stop to get it filled. I'm sorry. We'll do that on the way home."

"Nonsense," Sandy countered. "We can eat our lunch first. Later you can run to the pharmacy without me while I straighten up the house."

"No," he said firmly. "Wherever we go, it will be together till you get back to normal."

"You're afraid for me?" She was getting anxious again. "Why? What else did the doctor tell you?"

"Nothing much."

"Wade..."

"All right. He said you might fade in and out."

"Meaning?"

"Meaning you may experience further confusion before you're well."

"Is that dangerous?"

Her dazed, scared expression touched him so deeply he wanted to bend over and kiss away the worry lines till he and Sandy both lost their sense of time and place. "No," he said, giving her shoulders a comforting, reassuring squeeze. "Not as long as I'm here to take care of you."

She laid her cheek on his chest, marveling that their rapid heartbeats seemed to be synchronous. "I love you, Wade," she whispered. "All I want to do is go home."

In response, she felt his arms tighten around her, holding her even closer, and she thrilled to the arousal she could feel pressed against her abdomen. As soon as she could convince her cautious husband that she was well enough to celebrate recovery, she vowed they were going to have a wondrous night in bed. A second honeymoon.

Sandy smiled. That was the best idea she'd had for as long as she could remember.

Chapter Six

Slouched in the corner of the living-room sofa, Sandy awoke just as the sun was setting. Rubbing her eyes, she sat up slowly.

Wade was lounging in a reclining chair across the room, reading, but he lowered the paperback novel when he noticed she was aware of him. "Hello."

"Hi," she said, shaking her head slightly. "Wow. Those pills the doctor prescribed were powerful."

"They did seem to knock you out. How's the headache?"

She blinked to try to orient herself to the room and its contents. "Better. Oh-oh. I forgot to call my mother as I promised."

"I took care of that for you."

"Thanks. Did I ever finish lunch?"

"Nope. But at least you didn't fall asleep in your lasagna."

"That's good." She smiled over at him. "I hope you saved it. I'm famished."

Nodding, he laid aside his book and crossed the room to join her on the sofa in spite of his inner warnings to keep his distance for the sake of his overworked libido. It was one thing to be aware of impending disaster and quite another to reason one's way past it, wasn't it?

The problem seemed to be that *this* Sandy was the personification of the woman he had fallen in love with in the first place, not the individual she had become soon after their ill-fated marriage. Maybe he had pushed her too hard for commitment, he thought, recalling those early months as man and wife and the dire consequences of their otherwise unblemished love. Maybe if he hadn't insisted on a quick wedding they could have survived as a couple and successfully grown old together the way he'd always imagined.

She saw the pain reflected in his brooding gaze. "What is it, Wade? What's the matter?"

"It's nothing. I was just thinking."

"About me? Well, don't worry. You told me I'd be fine. That was the truth, wasn't it?"

"Yes."

"Then there's nothing to worry about." She began to smile. "So, let's go nuke leftovers in the microwave." Rising, she bent to place an affectionate kiss on his beard-shadowed cheek in passing.

The moment was so perfect, so ethereal, Wade couldn't help himself. He grasped her wrist and pulled her into his lap in one fluid motion. The surprise and joy on Sandy's face and the immediate way she responded only served to strengthen the erotic bond between them. At that particular instant, he didn't care about anything except having her in his arms and reliving the magic that was such a vivid part of his dreams.

She caught her breath. This was more like it! There was hunger in Wade's eyes beyond any she could remember and, happily, she could remember plenty. Wiggling into a more

comfortable, more intimate position, she threw her arms
around his neck and kissed him soundly on the mouth,
hoping her aggressiveness wouldn't turn him off.

To her utmost delight, his response was an explosion of
unbridled passion! Pulling her tightly to his body and
pressing her lips so hard with his that they tingled, he slid his
hand up her thigh and under the cuff of her loose, nylon
shorts, caressing, touching her heated skin as if he had been
deprived of lovemaking for an eternity.

Sandy moaned with lust and longing. Her mind spun,
freeing her subconscious. Wade *did* love her after all!

The idea that he might have ceased to do so took her by
complete surprise. Clinging to him, writhing to bring them
both closer to the moment of ultimate belonging, she fought
to banish the errant thought from her mind. Of course her
husband loved her. What was the matter with her? She had
never doubted his devotion and fidelity, had she?

He began touching her with a practiced zeal she could
hardly bear, totally obliterating any questions she might be
entertaining about their relationship. Nothing was wrong.
Nothing could be. Not when they could come together like
this and feel this way without any slower preliminaries.
Theirs was a lusty marriage with the tenderness of two people who cared so deeply they needed nothing else but each
other.

Abandoning the last of her doubts, she arched into his
palm in a syncopation he immediately echoed. Hard as an
iron rod beneath her hips, his manhood pressed into her,
while his fingers performed their own kind of magic.

When he broke away from her demanding kisses and
lowered his mouth to tease her breasts through the thin fabric of the shirt, she threw back her head and closed her eyes
against the light, totally lost in the pure ecstasy of the sen-
sations sizzling through her body.

She was close to fulfillment, so eager and ready she could
hardly reason, yet she wanted to share the pinnacle of her

passionate feelings with Wade. Making herself act, she reached down and covered the back of his hand with hers, barely able to speak.

"Stop. I want us to be together first."

His mouth was still nuzzling her breasts as he muttered, "Oh, Sandy..."

"Please," she begged, her voice breathless and husky from desire. "I want you to make love to me, Wade."

She felt him tense and begin to withdraw, but she didn't dream he would abruptly set her off his lap and jump to his feet the way he did. Waiting for him to strip and return to lie beside her on the sofa, she was astounded when he started for the door. "Wade?"

He didn't turn to look at her. "If you need me, I'll be outside, having a smoke," he said, clearing his throat as if he had a bad cold.

"You don't smoke, do you?" she asked, still befuddled at his strange behavior.

Wade muttered a curse. "I'm going to start."

"But what about us?"

He wanted to whirl and deny there was any such thing as *us* for the two of them, but he knew that would be a lie. The musky odor of desire still filled the room, making his head spin, his heart pound and his body remain taut and ready. If he stayed near her and she once again appealed to him to take her as his wife, he didn't know if he could walk away.

"I'll be on the porch," he said firmly, opening the door and stepping outside. "If you get hungry before I get back, go ahead and eat without me." At that, he slammed the door behind him, leaving Sandy alone in the silent room.

Tears of rejection and frustration filled her eyes. What had she done wrong? Always before, Wade had responded beautifully to her pleas for him to make love to her, so why was this time different? She licked her dry lips, thinking, wondering, trying to remember what she had said that might have affected him so adversely, but no answer came to her.

In self-defense, she began to imagine anything, everything, that might have so thoroughly destroyed the glorious mood of the evening.

Was it her disheveled appearance in the loose-fitting clothing she had borrowed from him? she wondered. Did he suddenly open his eyes and find her so much less attractive than before that he didn't want to have her in his bed? Or was it her hair? She did seem to recall that Wade had expressed a preference for long hair and hers was shorter than it had been when they'd met. Sandy ran her fingers through the soft waves. Surely the length of her hair couldn't make him walk away from a clear invitation to make love, could it?

She sighed and wiped the sparse tears from her cheeks. Negative thoughts like these were getting her nowhere. She never had understood men, starting with her own father. Obviously not much had changed in that regard.

Hugging her knees to her chest, she curled up on the couch and closed her eyes. In her memory, it was the spring of the year, her senior year in high school. She and Jane Ellen Peters, her best friend, were trying on their caps and gowns for graduation and discussing their respective fathers. Sandy was trying not to give in to feelings of self-pity.

"He said he'd be here on time," she told Jane.

"Then he will be." The other girl was taller than Sandy and painfully thin below a mop of curly, dark hair, but other than physical differences they could have been sisters, their ways of thinking and behaving were so similar.

"I don't know," Sandy said. "Remember that time in our freshman year when we were in the drama club play and he didn't come the way he promised?"

"He was stuck in the airport at Frankfurt, wasn't he?"

Sandy nodded. She was looking at her friend by focusing on their dual reflections in the oval vanity mirror. "Europe was having a terrible storm or something and all the planes were grounded."

"Well? See?" Jane Ellen held out her scrawny arms to emphasize her point. "He couldn't help it."

"He could have planned ahead and gotten here a few days early."

"I suppose so. But he does go all over the world on business and he usually gets back on time, doesn't he?"

"I guess." Sandy was pouting. "It's just that..."

"What?"

"Well, your father is always there when you need him. I wish mine were like that."

"At least you have a mother."

"So do you."

Jane Ellen tossed her hairbrush onto the bed and made a face at Sandy. "I have a stepmother."

"Same thing. I'd trade mine for yours in a minute."

"Yeah." The taller girl patted Sandy gently on the shoulder. "Sorry. I forgot about your mom's problems."

"How could you? You've seen her when she's drunk. It's pathetic." Sandy's jaw clenched. "I'm never going to be like her, I swear."

"You mean an alcoholic? I sure hope not."

"That, too," Sandy explained, picking up the brush to smooth back her long, golden brown hair while she talked. "What I meant was, I'm never going to be stuck in the house all day just waiting for a man to come home the way she does."

"I've wondered about that." Jane took back the brush. "Turn around." She began to run it through Sandy's hair while they continued to make eye contact in the mirror. "Why doesn't she go out and get a job the way my stepmother did when she got bored? I don't think she makes much of a salary, but at least it keeps her happy."

Sandy crossed her legs for comfort as she sat on the bed. "I've asked Mother, lots of times, and she always says the same thing—she gave up her formal education in order to

marry Dad, and that's why she isn't qualified to do anything worthwhile."

"You don't believe that, do you?"

"Sure. Why not? It's no sin to want a decent job, is it?"
Jane Ellen shook her head. "I guess not."

"That's why I'm so determined to finish getting a good
education, even if my father does think a college degree is a
useless waste for a woman."

"Did he actually say that?"

Sandy pouted again and stared at the disgusted-looking
sight in the mirror for a few seconds before breaking into a
smile. "No. But my mother has asked him to help out with
my tuition and he's refused. There's nothing more I can say
to convince him."

"You could always beg and plead and cry. It usually
works for me."

Chuckling, Sandy shot her friend a look of mock disdain. "I won't grovel for anybody, and you shouldn't, either. We're both on the honor roll for every semester this
year and most of the other ones since we started school.
We're smart. We can better ourselves without anybody's
help and you know it."

"Darned right!"

Seated on the sofa in the darkening living room, Sandy
found herself smiling again. Dear Jane Ellen. What a great
friend she was. Coming fully back to the current moment,
she opened her eyes, gazed around the unfamiliar room she
found herself sitting in and blinked hard to clear her head.

Natural light was almost gone, giving the surroundings a
ghostly glow and making the hair on the back of Sandy's
neck prickle. She briskly rubbed her arms. They were covered in goose flesh. This was spooky. Not only did she not
know where she was, but she couldn't remember leaving her
best friend's house after they had discussed graduation and
going on to college.

Getting slowly to her feet, Sandy noted that her limbs were slightly achy and her head had begun to throb. Maybe she had the flu. Holding her head, she peered down at her clothing. None of what she was wearing was hers. What was going on? Where was she? How had she gotten here?

Her mouth felt dry, her body flushed and trembling. Nervous and unsure what to do next, she rubbed her sweaty palms together while she tried to sort out the terrifying confusion she was feeling.

Suddenly only one goal seemed important. She had to get out of there and try to find her way home, no matter what. She started for the one door she could see, then stopped short. Suppose nobody was home at her house? Or what if her mother was drunk again? What then?

Jane Ellen's! That was where she could go to find out what was going on. There wasn't a single part of her life she hadn't shared with her best friend. When it seemed that nobody understood or cared, Jane Ellen was always there for her.

Moving again before she'd decided how she was going to get to her friend's house from goodness knows where, she rushed to the door, yanked it open and sprinted out onto the porch and down the stairs. In her peripheral vision, she noted a big man standing in the shadows, who made a grab at her as she passed.

She screamed as his fingers grazed her arm. "No! Let go!"

"Where do you think you're going?"

Successfully dodging his lunging grasp, she stumbled on the walkway, caught herself with one hand, then regained her equilibrium and began to run as fast as she could.

Wade was taken totally by surprise. His mind had been focused on their near lovemaking, and he was trying to think of someone they both knew who would be qualified and willing to take Sandra in until she recovered.

There was little noise behind him to signal her presence and she flew past him with such speed he had only a brief opportunity to make a grab for her and literally no chance to try to reason away whatever unfounded fears were making her flee.

So much for letting somebody else care for her, he thought, breaking into a run and following her past the end of his driveway and on down the block. The lady was in good physical shape and in a panic besides, giving her even more ready energy than normal. He was having no trouble keeping up with her, but he didn't know of anyone else—Violet, for instance—who could hope to do as well.

Wade saw Sandy slow, look both ways, then turn south along Magnolia. It seemed that she was headed for the old neighborhood, near the high school, and he wondered what demons were driving her to go there.

Clearly she was tiring. He slowed his pace to drop back and keep from frightening her more. Considering the way she had looked at him in the instant he'd made a grab for her, she didn't remember who he was. Under those circumstances, Wade figured he could do her more good by staying in the background and simply letting her work out her confusion alone than he could by confronting her. Besides, as long as she was safe there was little more he dared do without chancing arrest for kidnapping or assault. He couldn't watch over her from a jail cell, now could he?

Her sides heaving, Sandy finally paused at the front of an old brownstone, then started quickly for the front door. Wade stepped to one side of the property and stood partially hidden by a thick, squat, blue-green cypress. He'd remain secreted till he saw the outcome of Sandy's quest, and then decide what to do next. Hopefully she'd come to her senses and he wouldn't have to interfere at all.

"Jane Ellen," she called, pounding on the door. "Jane, open up!"

Wade could hear her voice clearly and the name triggered his memory. Of course! Jane Peters, her high-school confidante and maid of honor at their wedding. Maybe the other woman would volunteer to help when she learned what was wrong. He sure hoped so, for both his sake and Sandy's.

Sandy was shouting, her fists beating on the heavy mahogany door. "Jane Ellen! Please. It's me! Let me in."

The door eased open, its full swing hindered by a visible safety chain. "What do you want?" a woman's voice asked.

"Mrs. Peters? It's me, Sandy McNamara. Let me in. I have to talk to Jane."

"There's nobody here by that name," the woman said. She was peering through the narrow opening with one eye. "Go away."

"But... I know she lives here. We go to Riverside High together."

"I don't have any kids, lady, and I don't know what you're trying to pull. You may think you can fool me, but I can tell you haven't been in high school for years. You'd better come up with a better story than that if you expect to be believed." She started to close the door.

Sandy leaned on it with all her remaining strength. "Wait. There has to be a mistake. I know this is the right house. I come here after school all the time."

The door slammed. Dejected and thoroughly disheartened, Sandy turned back to the street just in time to see a tall, broad-shouldered man step out from behind some bushes and start up the steps toward her.

It was the same man who had tried to capture her before! It had to be. There was an ominous familiarity about him that crept into her bones and gave her a sick, weak, dizzy feeling.

Sandy tensed, preparing to defend herself and having absolutely no idea how to ward off an attack. This couldn't be happening. Not to her. She'd never harmed another living soul in her whole life.

The man took a step closer. Then another. Feeling as if she were trapped in a horrific nightmare, she gasped in a quick breath and opened her mouth to scream.

Wade clasped his hand over her mouth as he grabbed her, saw the momentary terror in her eyes and caught her as she collapsed in his arms, unconscious.

He picked her up, placed a kiss on her forehead, carried her down the stairs and started home. "Oh, honey, I'm so sorry I scared you," he said, knowing she couldn't hear him and talking merely to salve his conscience. "I didn't know what else to do to keep you from screaming. All we need is for somebody to call the cops and have me thrown in jail. By the time I talked my way out, you could be lost or in worse trouble and I might never find you again."

Which would be for the best, his logical subconscious added. Wade didn't argue. Some women were cut out for white picket fences and a peaceful family life and some weren't. If he hadn't been so head over heels in love when he'd talked Sandy into an early marriage, he would have seen how dedicated she was to making a successful career her primary goal. He sighed. In retrospect, he could see he was probably as much to blame for some of their conflicts as she was.

"I loved you so much, Sandra Walker," he whispered against the silkiness of her windblown hair. "So much."

Sandy felt his muscular arms tighten around her and she opened her eyes, looking up at his strong, square jaw. "I love you, too, Wade," she purred. "Where are we going?"

He paused in his purposeful striding. *Thank God.* She was back to recognizing him. "You're awake?"

"Mmm-hmm." She glanced at their surroundings. "What are we doing out here?"

"It's a long story, Sandy. Just relax and I'll have you home in no time."

Threading one arm around his neck, she cuddled closer, reveling in the strength of his body and the sanctuary of his embrace. "I don't care where I am as long as I'm with you," she said.

Chapter Seven

It took all the self-control Wade could muster to keep from setting her on her feet immediately and trying to explain what was really going on. Not that it would help, he told himself. If Sandy didn't get back to normal soon, her illness was bound to drive him crazy no matter what he did.

And the way she was clinging to him! So loving. So trusting. It tore at his soul to remember similar times they'd shared, before...

Recalling the precise reasons for their breakup, he hardened his heart against letting himself care for her the way he once had. Never again would he make the mistake of totally trusting another woman, no matter how innocent or lovely she was. He'd been there. Done that. And the disappointment it had caused had hurt like hell.

He took her by the arm and started off for his house. "Come with me and I'll try to explain what is happening to you, okay?"

"Where's Matilda? Why don't we drive?"

The old Mustang again. He grimaced. "That car got wrecked a long time ago. It's part of the story I need to tell you when we get home."

"Wrecked? But what happened? I know how you loved that old car."

"Yeah, well, that's the way things go sometimes. You can't always keep the things you love the most." His jaw muscles clenched.

Sandy gazed up at him through a haze of confusion and building distress. Somehow she could tell he was no longer referring to the yellow Mustang convertible they had named Matilda early in their courtship. His countenance was hard, unforgiving, as if he were holding a grudge against her that extended all the way to his core. But why? What had happened between them? And why had he called her Sandra Walker when she was positive they weren't married yet?

"Wade?" She fell into step beside him as he started off, taking three steps for every two of his.

"What?"

"Are we still happy together? Please tell me."

He snorted with disdain. "Happy? Sandy, I don't know about you, but I don't think I've been truly happy since right before you graduated college."

"I did?" Pausing, she scowled. "You mean to tell me I went all through college and I don't remember any of it?"

"That's not the half of it," he said with a self-denigrating chuckle.

"Wade, stop this. Don't tease. You're scaring me." She took his hand and held tight for moral support, relieved when he didn't shake off her touch.

"I'm not teasing, Sandra," he said with a sigh and a perfunctory squeeze of her slim fingers. "Believe me, I wish to heaven I was."

By the time they reached Wade's house, he was having to carry Sandy once more. Her head had begun to pound and she was in so much pain he couldn't help worrying. Settling her on the bed, he called the clinic once again, disgusted when they merely reiterated their earlier diagnosis and recommended the same treatment. Wade gave her the prescribed medication and sat with her while it took effect.

"We can't go on like this," he said, hoping she was cognizant enough to understand. "You have to make an appointment to see your regular doctor."

Sandy rubbed her aching temples. "Dr. Schwartz. My mother knows his number. You should call her anyway, Wade, and tell her I'm all right so she doesn't worry when I don't come home tonight."

"You really want to stay here with me?" Part of him was hoping she'd say no.

"Of course I do. You know what it's like at my house. I'd be lucky to get an aspirin, let alone the TLC you're giving me." She gazed over at him, her eyes half-closed, her breathing slow and steady. "I trust you to behave yourself."

"Can I trust you?" he countered.

Sandy managed a smile through the haze of pain. "Nope."

Rising, he drew a blanket over her and stood, looking down. "Rest. I'll be in the next room if you need me."

Her plea was faint but nonetheless compelling. "Stay with me, Wade. Please? I know I'm probably not making much sense, but I feel scared all the time unless I'm with you."

"It's just because of the bump you got on the head, as I already explained," he told her calmly. "You'll be back to normal soon and all this will seem like a bad dream."

"It already does." She covered her eyes to blot out the painful light from the bedside lamp. "Tell me again why I was blocks away from here."

"You were looking for an old friend. Don't bother yourself about that now. Sleep. You'll feel better in the morning."

"You won't leave me?"

Wade shook his head as he watched her drift closer and closer to the deep, untroubled sleep the medication allowed her to have. "No," he said soberly. "I won't leave you. I'll be close by if you need me."

She sighed. "Oh, good. I love you so much, Wade. I really do."

"I know," he said. It was depressing to realize she was referring to emotional ties from their past, not the present. It hurt like the devil to hear her expound on the wonderful life they had once had and lost. He grimaced, steeling himself for whatever came next. This time warp of Sandy's was getting harder and harder to bear.

"One more day," Wade muttered. "I'll hold out one more day, and then I'm going to do *something,* even if it's difficult for both of us."

As he stood over her, watching, her breathing evened out, her expression relaxing into one of heavenly peace. Wade waited a few minutes more, just to be certain she was fully asleep, then turned out the light and quietly left the room, determined to find constructive activities to help take his mind off Sandra's lithe body curled up so invitingly on his bed.

Going through the house with purposeful alacrity, he wadded the latest newspapers into a rumpled ball, punched the sofa pillows back into place where she had lain earlier, then grabbed up the clothing she'd left in the spare bathroom, as if to erase every trace of her from his home.

The discarded clothing still carried her sweet scent, he noted, disgusted with himself for paying attention to such a sexually arousing detail. Not that he could avoid such things. After all, he was only in his early thirties and far from over-the-hill in the romance department.

"Hah!" Wade announced to the empty room. What made him think he wasn't? He hadn't had a serious relationship since he and Sandy had gotten divorced.

"Because of the way I'm starting to feel about her," he countered. "And for once, I wish I wasn't having the reactions of a normal man."

But he was. In spades. And in the morning, when Sandy awoke, he was going to have to decide how much to tell her regarding their failed marriage and the life she had gone on to make for herself. To begin with, he supposed he could take her to her apartment in the hope that seeing it would shock her out of her memory loss. At least that way she could pick up a few personal items, too.

Sighing in disgust, Wade looked down at the crumpled clothing he was still holding and quickly tossed it into the washing machine with some of his own things. The way his nerves were singing and his adrenaline pumping, there would be plenty of time to see the garments through all the necessary wash-and-dry cycles and get in twenty or thirty reps of heavy lifts with a barbell, too.

After that, he'd probably throw in a hundred push-ups and some bicep curls for good measure. One thing he knew for sure—he'd have to burn off a lot more excess energy before he'd be able to calm down enough to turn in for the night and actually expect to sleep.

His gut tightened in a spasm of pure longing. Going to bed meant he'd be spending another eight sleepless hours lying next to Sandy and wishing he were half as disoriented as she.

Cursing, Wade turned on the washing machine and stomped back down the hall to check on his houseguest.

Sandy sensed the moment he lay down beside her. Reaching over, she touched the bare skin of his back, her fingertips tracing the contours of his muscles with relish. Life was glorious. Such perfect happiness seemed too good to be true, as if she were cheating fate by usurping more joy than any one person was entitled to.

Then, insidiously, her pleasure began to fade and feelings of loss filled her. A dense cloud of fog drifted closer to envelop her, shrouding the sight of Wade and their marital bed till she could no longer see anything through the thick veil.

Voices, Sandy thought. *I hear voices.* They were shouting and cursing, their vehemence unquestioned. She strained to hear. It was Wade! And he sounded as if he were furious with someone.

Sandy saw herself, dressed in a black robe, coming down from the podium after having received her college degree. Instead of applauding her accomplishment, the onlookers were all staring at her, shouting epithets and angrily shaking their fists!

She looked closer, hoping to recognize at least one friend in the crowd. Gasping, she realized every person there was made in the image of Wade and *all* of them were yelling at her. But why?

Pelted with rotten fruit, she dodged to cover her face and try to escape. The mob surged around her. Trying to make sense of their savage cries and thereby offer some defense, she found she was unable to sort out the mingled threats and accusations. All she could tell was that something dreadful had happened and it was apparently her fault.

"I'm sorry!" Sandy cried. "I didn't mean it. Why are you doing this to me?"

Lying beside her, Wade reached across the wide bed and touched her shoulder to calm her.

Arms flailing, she fought him. Tears of remorse slid from the corners of her eyes to wet her golden brown hair and the pillow beneath. This was wrong! All wrong. She hadn't done anything bad, so why did they all think she had? And why were they trying to restrain her? What horrid fate did they have in mind as her punishment?

"Sandy. Stop it. It's me," Wade said, holding her arms so she couldn't hurt herself or him.

She was growing hysterical. Tossing her head from side to side, she sobbed and pleaded with him to let her go. "No! It's not my fault. It's not. Don't you see?"

Wade didn't know what demons were currently haunting her tortured mind, but he saw no reason to deny her the solace she so evidently needed. "I know it's not." He was almost shouting in order to be heard over her loud weeping. "It's okay, Sandy. You're safe. I'm here."

Pulling her into his arms, he held her till she quieted more. "Hush. You had a bad dream, that's all. It's over."

Her eyelids fluttered, then lifted. Seeing Wade and hearing his calming voice, she threw her arms around him and gripped him with all the strength left in her weary body. "Oh, thank God."

"You must have been having an awful nightmare to set you off like that. Want to tell me about it?" Stroking her hair, he held her and listened to her breathing begin to return to normal.

She rubbed her eyes and sniffled. "I don't remember much, only that everybody was trying to punish me."

"For what?"

"I don't know. I can't think of a single thing I ever did to anyone that would make me feel so guilty and helpless, can you?"

Wade decided this was not the proper time to tell her that he could indeed recall such an event. It would serve no purpose to dredge up their unhappy past, especially since Sandy was obviously far from back to normal. One crisis at a time, real or otherwise, was plenty.

He merely shook his head. "Better get some sleep. I have a big day planned for us tomorrow."

"Is it the weekend?"

"No. Tomorrow's Tuesday. Why?"

"Because I have to go to work."

He tensed, hoping she was referring to her current job as a financial consultant for a brokerage firm in San Bernardino. "Oh? Where?"

Sandy poked him in the ribs and gave him a droll look. "As if you didn't know."

"Humor me. It's been a rough night."

"Mrs. Lynch's first-grade class at Rossmore Elementary, of course. Instructional aides don't make much money, I know, but I can't expect you to pay off all my student loans, even though you have offered."

Wade couldn't tell if Sandy was thinking prenuptials or postnuptials. He eyed her cautiously. If she thought they were husband and wife again, no telling what she would propose they do next.

He decided to try to distract her. "How's your head?"

"Now that you mention it . . ." She pressed her fingertips to her temples, then threaded them through her tousled hair. "Ouch! There's a bump on my head. How did that get there?"

"You fell off your mountain bike."

"I did?" She paused, frowning at him. "Wait a minute. I don't have a mountain bike."

"You do now."

Sandy raised herself on one elbow and stared at him. "Whoa. I ought to know if I own a bicycle or not."

"You're right. You ought to," Wade told her. "As a matter of fact, there are a lot of things you ought to know that have slipped out of your memory."

"There are?"

"Uh-huh."

"Prove it."

"Not now." Swinging his legs off the opposite side of the bed, he got to his feet. "Just relax. I'll go get you another pill and some juice."

Sandy mirrored his actions, finding that her balance left a bit to be desired when she stood. She paused, wondering

why she'd felt such a surge of pure panic at the thought of
Wade leaving her side, even for a few minutes.

Circling the bed, he grasped her shoulders and held her
while she looked up into his eyes with a gaze that demanded better explanations. "Don't treat me like an inva-
lid, Wade. I can go with you."

"No, you can't. You've been dizzy and disoriented. Stay
here and be good, will you?"

"No." Hands on her hips, she faced him firmly.

"I'm just going to the kitchen, Sandra. I'm not leaving
you. I swear."

She managed a smile. "I know that. And I believe it in my
head. It's the rest of me that feels strange about letting you
out of my sight."

Seeing that he was not going to win, Wade gave up arguing and took her hand. "Okay. Come on."

Warmed by his touch and not put off by the stern tone of
voice he was using, she noted the familiar feel of his skin,
the strength of his fingers, the breadth of his palm where it
spanned hers and then some.

They'd held hands like that in a churchlike setting, she
recalled, unsure where or when but totally convinced that
her basic perception was correct. It had happened in the
spring, she remembered, only they weren't in an actual re-
ligious sanctuary, they were outside. The sun was shining
and it was a balmy, lovely day. She remembered being
nervous then, too, although she couldn't imagine why.

Sandy grasped Wade's fingers more tightly for moral
support as she accompanied him into the kitchen. They were
both barefoot. Other than that, she was fully dressed in the
middle of the night. So was Wade. How odd.

"Um, honey?" She tugged on his hand.

"What?"

"When did we start going to bed with our clothes on?"

He made a guttural sound of disgust. "Since you hit your
head."

"Oh. Well, I'm better now, and I want to take a shower and get comfortable before we go back to sleep." Undoing the buttons on the front of the oversized shirt she was wearing, she let the garment fall open and hang loose all the way to the hem.

Wade turned his back so he wouldn't be tempted to look at the soft swell of her breasts as she bared them. "You can use one of my T-shirts for a nightgown, if you want. They should be long enough to be decent."

"I have my own nightie. You know I only steal your T-shirts when we're out camping and my shoulders get too cold."

"Right." He leaned his hands on the kitchen counter next to the sink, waiting for her to leave the room. If he turned around now, he was afraid the sight of Sandy's womanly curves would cost him the last shred of self-control he possessed. Neither of them could afford that.

She laid her cheek in the middle of his back and hugged him from behind. "We did have some great times in the woods on our honeymoon, didn't we?"

"Yeah." Embarrassed that his whole body was trembling from her closeness, Wade shut his eyes against the reality of her soft breasts pressed to his back, the nipples hardening the way he remembered they always had when Sandy was in the mood for love.

"Go take your shower," he ordered gruffly. "I'll bring your pills and something warm to wear, okay?"

Hesitantly she released him and stepped away. "Okay, if you say so, but I expect you to join me."

"Not this time, Sandra," he said.

Her voice was a quiet purr, vibrating with desire, as she asked, "When?" fully expecting him to give in and decide to shower with her the way he always used to.

Instead she heard him say, "Never," and in her fast-pounding, broken heart she suddenly knew this was not the first time Wade had denied her the love and affection she so desperately needed.

Turning away from the pain of his rejection and the terror of the bitter memories dancing wildly on the fringes of her consciousness, she dashed down the hall into the master bathroom and slammed the door behind her.

Chapter Eight

Sandy stood under the water in the shower for what seemed like forever and let it beat against her face to wash away the tears. No matter how hard she tried, she couldn't make sense of the feelings of emptiness that threatened to overwhelm her. Bits and pieces of conversations and events tumbled through her mind, never quite clear, never quite there, hardly more than faint, ambiguous impressions.

She turned off the water and reached for a towel. There was no use fighting to remember things when her head was pounding so. If the bump on her scalp really was the reason for her confusion, then surely it would pass. All she really wanted to know at the moment was why Wade was acting so strangely. It was as though she didn't know him anymore.

Rubbing herself dry, she ignored the scrape on her elbow as she glanced around the bathroom. Everything looked exactly the way she remembered it, except for the absence of the overgrown houseplants she had nurtured in there since she and Wade had begun living together as man and wife. The humidity in a bathroom was perfect for the Boston ferns, schefflera and dieffenbachia she'd had hanging from hooks in the ceiling by the window or stacked in the corners of the wide, faux-marble counter surrounding the twin sinks.

Funny, she thought, pausing to study the gold-flecked tiles on the floor. The plant hooks were still in place, but there wasn't even one tiny, brown leaf from the Boston fern's thick plumage lurking below. That alone was a rarity. The darned thing shed worse than a long-haired pet dog most of the time.

A sharp knock on the door startled her. Since they were alone in the house, she knew her caller had to be Wade, but why in heavens did he think he needed to knock?

Holding her towel to her chest with one hand while letting most of the terry cloth hang down on either side of her body, she flung open the door. The immediate look of wanton lust erasing Wade's stern expression made her doubt all her other tenuous conclusions. Things might not be exactly as they once were between them, but at least his hunger for her had not waned.

"I brought you a clean T-shirt to wear," he said, never taking his eyes off her.

"Thanks." Sandy would rather have had one of her satin gowns, but she decided not to protest his sincere efforts to care for her the way he felt was best.

Neither of them moved. "I hoped you might change your mind and join me," she said in a near whisper. "I really do wish you had."

Wade shook his head, then ran the fingers of one hand through his thick, dark hair. He had to move, to distract himself, or they were both going to be sorry. "Get dressed," he said abruptly. "I put your pills and a glass of juice on the nightstand by the bed."

"Thanks." Frozen by his mesmerizing gaze, Sandy waited, willing him to take her in his arms and kiss away all her cares, both real and imagined.

"You'd better dry off before you catch a chill." His voice had mellowed, as if the telling look on his handsome face had finally gained control of the rest of his stern persona.

Turning slowly, Sandy presented her bare back to him and handed him the towel. "Dry me?"

Before he had a chance to think better of it, Wade had the damp towel in his grasp and had stepped closer. His hand was shaking when he reached for her, he noted with disdain. No wonder. Droplets of water shimmered on Sandy's back, some of them sliding down along the curve of her waist to the smooth swelling of her hips, others glistening in place, beckoning to his hands, his touch.

She lifted her hair off her shoulders and held it out of the way to further urge him to continue stroking the soft toweling over her skin. Soon he would give in and make love to her, she knew. He'd have to. This was too perfect a moment to ignore, no matter what personal problems they may or may not have had before.

Sighing, she closed her eyes, her body swaying slightly from his tender ministrations. "Um. That feels wonderful."

"I know," Wade said. Hesitating only briefly, he lowered his head and placed a kiss on the back of her neck. She tasted of soap and sweetness, her natural perfume an intoxicating aphrodisiac. Hard and ready, he cast the towel aside and freed his hands to encircle her ribs, coming to rest on the fullness of her breasts. The moment his fingers grazed the tips of her nipples, she moaned in ecstasy and leaned back against him, intensifying the eroticism of the moment.

"Oh, Sandy..."

"I know. I need you, too," she said, pressing her hips to his till she could feel every inch of his undeniable desire. Not willing to give up her temporary advantage, she wriggled against him, knowing just such a movement was guaranteed to drive him wild.

Wade's hands left her straining breasts, slid down the curve of her waist and came to rest on the bones of her hips so he could hold her to him as he thrust forward in like cadence. Part of him was pretending it didn't matter what they did as long as Sandy was willing, and he almost had himself believing it. Almost, but not quite.

He would break off their sizzling contact and let her go soon, he told himself. Just a few more minutes of pleasure, a few more beats of his racing heart, a fleeting chance to recapture the sense of happiness and fulfillment he had found only in the past and only with her.

Sandy let go of her hair, reached down and covered the backs of his hands with her palms, urging him on. If he wasn't still clad in his jeans, she knew they would already be joined. Why didn't he stop long enough to remove the only physical barrier to their lovemaking?

Beginning with the curve of her shoulder, Wade kissed his way up to her neck, nuzzling her behind the ear till she thought she would go mad. His hips were still grinding against hers, his manhood threatening to burst through the fabric of his jeans.

No longer willing to be patient, Sandy slid her right hand behind her, slipped it between them and began fiddling with the buttons on his fly. Wade didn't help, she noticed, but neither did he object.

Her fingers slipped the first button loose, then another and another till he was free. This was more like it, she thought, curling her hand around his shaft through the thin covering of his shorts. She shivered with excitement and expectation. This was Wade, her Wade, and he wanted her as much as she wanted him.

Her temples were still pounding, especially since she'd gotten so aroused. Her headache beat furiously and made her weak in the knees but she refused to yield to its intrusive pain. There was more at stake at this moment than personal comfort. Much more. It made no difference to Sandy that she didn't know what had gone wrong in her marriage; she was certain that once they made love the way they used to, everything would be all right.

Turn me around and sweep me up in your arms, she thought, wishing she dared speak the desire aloud. Or they could even have sex just as they stood. Sandy didn't care. As long as she belonged to Wade once again, that was all that mattered.

Then, her reckless fantasy began to come true! He lifted her across his chest and held her close.

The damp towel fell to the floor, forgotten. This was the very same romantic scenario she had conjured up in her vivid imagination, and it was unfolding as if she had somehow wished it to being.

In five purposeful strides Wade was across the room and standing by the side of the bed. Sandy closed her eyes and clung to him, knowing the next few minutes would repair any wounds to their no longer blissful marriage.

Gently, Wade lowered her onto the mattress and released his hold, gazing at her with misty eyes. She was beautiful! And so innocent-looking, in spite of all he knew about her true character.

I loved you, once, he thought with a sigh.

Straightening, he forced himself to remember all the bad and cast aside the greater good, creating the harsh emotional reaction he had hoped for. It was barely adequate to enable him to retreat but it did suffice.

Sandy's eyes flew open the instant she sensed him leaving the room. Astounded, she watched Wade turn on his heel and stamp out into the hall, leaving her alone in the bed she had envisioned as the place they would renew their marriage vows and thereby get their lives back on track.

"Wait!" Her tremulous voice was weak and ineffectual as she called after him.

The door slammed.

Hugging herself against the cold his absence had intensified, Sandy pulled the covers up around her and held them tightly to her chest, wishing she were well again so she could be certain this wasn't all another bad dream.

A tear trickled down to dampen her cheek. If this was a dream, it sure was a lousy one.

Pacing the floor in the living room gave Wade little comfort. What he really wanted to do was go back into that bedroom and take all Sandy was offering and then some. He adjusted his clothing to try to take some of the pressure off his manhood but quickly decided it didn't matter what he wore or didn't wear. As long as that woman was in the house and needed his help, he wasn't going to be able to relax. Period.

Without considering how late it was, he picked up the telephone and punched in his brother's number. Art answered on the fifth ring, his "Hello" little more than a mumble.

"It's me, Wade."

"Jeez, Wade, it's 3:00 a.m.! What's wrong? You drunk?"

"Not yet."

"Is there a chance? Because if there is, I'm not coming down to city hall to bail you out again. I thought you were through with all that nonsense now that Sandy's gone."

"I was." He rubbed his bloodshot eyes. "I am. I haven't had a drink for two years."

"Then what's the matter?"

"Sandy's back." He heard shuffling in the background as his younger brother sat up in bed.

"She's *what?*"

"You heard me. She showed up here yesterday with some kind of head injury."

"Well, get rid of her, man."

"I can't." Wade took a deep breath and sighed. "She thinks we're still married."

"Yeah, right."

"No, she does. It's weird. I didn't believe it, either, till I took her to a doctor. He says she'll regain her memory of the present as soon as the swelling in her head goes down."

"And in the meantime?" Art asked.

Wade cursed. "In the meantime, I'm running around with a permanent bulge in my pants and she's acting like she'd love to get me into the sack."

"It could be worse," Art countered with a snide chuckle. "It could be the other way around."

"Oh, it is," Wade said. "I'd love to take her up on one of her offers. The trouble is, I'm having a devil of a time keeping in mind the reason I divorced her in the first place."

"Yeah, well, I never did understand the sordid details of that myself," the younger man said. "Are you sure it was all her fault?"

Hardening his heart, Wade said, "Hell, yes," evident anger emphasizing his words.

"Okay, okay. You don't have to snap at me. I'm on your side, remember?" Art waited in silence for a few long seconds. "So why are you calling me in the middle of the night?"

"Damned if I know. I just needed someone to talk to, I guess."

"Look, bro, this isn't one of those 900 numbers where you get to unburden your soul for three or four dollars a minute. Get real. If you expect me to keep the print shop running well while you loaf, I'm going to have to get some sleep. ¿*Comprende?*"

Wade scowled at the telephone as if Art were sitting there in its place. "Yeah, I get it. Sounds like you're seeing Maria again."

"Just because I slipped into Spanish?" He chuckled. "If you must know, she and I are getting pretty serious. What do you think the old man will say about that?"

"He'll have a fit, but so what? It's your life."

"Yeah. If I remember right, he didn't like Sandy, either."

"Except, in that particular case he was right." Wade glanced back toward the bedroom where he'd left her and tried to forget the frightened, forsaken expression on her face when he'd put her down and walked away.

"Maybe. Look," Art said, "do you want me to get dressed and come over there to defend you from your nasty urges?"

"That won't be necessary."

"You sure?" Art was chuckling under his breath. "It might be worth the trip just to see my big brother stuck in a situation he can't handle."

Wade muttered something crass he didn't intend for the younger man to hear before he said, "I can handle Sandra. You just keep our business afloat and don't look for me in the office till she's back to normal, okay?"

"Sure. Have a good time, bro."

"I'm having a hell of a time, or I wouldn't have admitted it to you and you know it."

"Yeah, well, as they say, what goes around, comes around."

"What's that supposed to mean?" Wade demanded.

"Just that you put Sandy through some pretty tough times a couple of years ago and maybe it's time for you to face up to what you did to her."

"Our divorce has nothing to do with her present condition. She hit her head. That's all."

"Fine. But think about this," Art said. "Of all the reactions she might have had to a head injury, why pick the most turbulent, unhappy time in her life and revert to that?"

"It wasn't all unhappy." The past day and a half with Sandy had reminded him of that poignant fact all too often.

"Aha! Now the truth comes out."

"You don't need to sound so superior, Art. I never claimed my marriage was that bad."

"Then why...?"

"You know damn well why."

"You still think she did it on purpose?"

Sighing, Wade raked his fingers through his hair. "I did."

"But you're not sure anymore?" The young man sounded hopeful.

"It doesn't matter," Wade said flatly. "Whatever chances at happiness Sandy and I once had are long gone and so is the love we felt for each other."

"Then why are you helping her?"

"Humph. That's a darned good question, kid. I guess, because she needs me. She doesn't have anybody else."

"So, find her somebody," Art suggested. "If you really don't want to get involved with her again, get busy and pick some other sucker to baby-sit her."

"I thought of that. I'm just afraid a stranger wouldn't take good enough care of her while she's so vulnerable."

Art was laughing loudly into the phone, his high humor echoing across the room as Wade held the receiver away from his ear to dim the noise.

"I *thought* so. You do still have a thing for her!"

Wade would have argued if he hadn't been so disgruntled to admit his outspoken brother was dead right.

Sandy swallowed the medication and juice Wade had left on the nightstand and was looking forward to an untroubled sleep. This time, though, the pills took longer than usual to calm her down and relieve the pounding pressure in her head.

Part of the problem was her racing mind, she knew, yet she wasn't able or willing to let go of the puzzling thoughts that haunted her. There had to be answers as well as more questions hidden in her subconscious memory. All she had to do was relax, concentrate, and everything would become clear.

Sure, she thought, her cynicism growing. *And while I'm at it, maybe I can figure out where my clothes and my favorite houseplants have gotten to, not to mention my driver's license and those old wallet-size photos I loved so much.*

Sandy made a face as she swung her legs over the side of the bed and stood up. *Fine. So I'm nuts. I can live with that as long as I have Wade.*

Only she apparently didn't have him anymore, did she? As inconceivable as the idea was, he had evidently thrown her away like an old pair of shoes, although why she couldn't imagine.

Padding back to the bathroom, she picked up the plain, white T-shirt he had loaned her and slipped it over her head, hugging herself when she had the long torso pulled down into place. Wade had been right; it did keep her decent, at least so long as she remained upright and dignified.

Which was a pretty safe bet at present, Sandy decided. She glanced at the empty, mussed bed and found she didn't want to return to it. Not all alone. There seemed to be no chance that Wade was going to change his mind and come looking for her there, so why bother to follow his orders? Besides, she wasn't really sleepy yet.

Walking to the door, she did have to admit her equilibrium was a bit shaky, not to mention the slight blurring of her vision. Oh, well. If she fell down in a heap and conked herself on the head again, maybe she'd regain the memory she'd lost and her life would start to make sense. *Yeah, right.*

Still a bit chilly, she rambled down the hall toward the kitchen in search of a cup of hot cocoa. Although a light was on there, she didn't see any reason to avoid Wade simply because he was mad at her. Let him rant and rave if it made him feel better. Who cared? Chin up, she padded into the kitchen.

"What are you doing up?" he asked, confronting her before she could even get to the refrigerator to see if they had any milk.

"Um..." Sandy blinked in the bright light of the recessed overhead fixtures. The answer to his question was right on the tip of her tongue. Or at least it had been. The problem was, her tongue was beginning to feel as fuzzy as her brain.

"Hot chocolate!" she announced, proud of herself for remembering.

"I don't have any."

Sandy was not going to be dissuaded. "Fine. Then I'll have a glass of warm milk, instead." Making her way to the cupboard beside the stove, she bent down to retrieve a small saucepan and temporarily lost her balance when a gigantic surge of pain filled her head. She caught herself on the rim of the tiled counter.

"You took your pill, didn't you?"

"Of course I did."

"You should be in bed," Wade told her. "You walk like you've been drinking."

"You know I don't drink." She didn't protest when he took the pan from her and placed it on the nearest burner.

"Go sit down, Sandra. I'll do this."

"I can take care of myself."

"In a pig's eye." He led her by the arm to the table, seeing that she was safely settled in a chair before returning to the task at hand.

"I can so. I got dressed by myself." Smoothing the long tail of the cotton shirt, she tugged it demurely over her thighs and tucked it into place beneath her hips to hold it there.

"Yeah, I noticed," Wade grumbled. "You don't pull any punches, do you?"

"I beg your pardon?" The room was starting to get darker, less distinct, and she wondered why her husband didn't turn on more lights. How could he see to cook under such trying circumstances?

"That shirt is thin and it clings to you, as if you didn't know."

"Don't blame me," she countered. "It's the one you gave me to wear."

"Not traipsing around the house!" His voice was rising noticeably and he'd begun to perspire. "It was supposed to keep you warm in bed, that's all."

"It's too lonesome in there," she said. "I don't like to be alone if I don't have to be."

Wade was not going to go into detail about why her presence in the revealing shirt bothered him so much. His mind, however, had listed and cataloged every curve, every swell and exactly where her hardened nipples touched the soft, white fabric. Yes, it was a plain, masculine garment but that didn't mean Sandy's shapely body was disguised beneath it. Oh, no. He bet she would have looked just as sexy in anything she put on.

Managing to glance away long enough to get the carton of milk out of the refrigerator, Wade poured some into the saucepan and lit the burner beneath it.

"How hot do you want this?" he asked over his shoulder. There was no answer. "Sandy...?"

She'd folded her arms on the table and laid her head on them like a pillow. Only luck had kept her from losing her balance and tumbling to the floor as she'd fallen asleep.

Wade shook his head in disbelief. He was either going to have to leave her there all night, which he clearly couldn't safely do, or he was going to have to carry her off to bed again.

Well, he thought, steeling himself for the onslaught to his senses, at least she was *partially* dressed this time.

Chapter Nine

Struggling with the constant fatigue brought on by her injury, Sandy was late awaking in the morning. One glance at the bedside clock told her she was going to have to hurry if she hoped to get to work on time.

Wade had obviously gotten up earlier, leaving her to sleep in, she thought, wondering why he'd bothered to lay out her clothes for the first time since their marriage.

She shrugged, shaking her head. The outfit draped carefully over the end of the bed was not one she would have necessarily chosen to wear that day. Nevertheless, it was sweet of him to try so hard to please her, and she wasn't about to disappoint him by looking for something else to wear when he had obviously gone to a lot of trouble to try to be accommodating.

Her jeans were clean and fresh-looking, as if they'd recently come from the dryer, and so was her pink-flowered blouse. Folded and neatly placed atop them were the brief, lacy undergarments she always wore to make herself feel most desirable.

Grabbing up the clothing and piling it on a chair, she stuck her head out the bedroom door and called to him. "Wade! You forgot to wake me. I'm late. Will you fix me some toast and coffee while I get dressed, please?"

Appearing in the kitchen door, his shirt sleeves rolled up to his elbows, his slacks a comfortable, casual cotton, he looked puzzled. "Late for what?"

"For work."

"You're not going to try to go to work."

"Who says I'm not?"

"I do."

She placed her hands on her hips, the action lifting the makeshift nightie almost to the tops of her thighs. "Don't be silly."

"I'm not the one with a head injury—you are." He forced himself to concentrate on her face while his peripheral vision took in the telling shadows at the hem of the shirt.

"So?"

"So what makes you think you'll be any good at your job if you do manage to get there today?"

"It's not like I'm a rocket scientist or an air-traffic controller," she countered. "I'm sure I can look after little kids, even if I am a bit slower than usual."

Crossing her arms in front of her, she lifted the oversize T-shirt over her head in one fluid sweep and tossed it aside. "So let's stop arguing and get going. I don't want to be tardy on my first day back." She was threading her arms through the straps of her bra and reaching behind her to fasten it while she talked.

Wade thought he was going to strangle her. There she stood, not at all concerned about her nakedness, while he, on the other hand, was quietly going mad with longing. Unwilling to look away, he watched her pull on her lacy panties and snug them up high on her hips.

Clearly she assumed they were still married. He licked his parched lips and tried to think of some way to find out how grounded in fact she currently was without making her afraid again. "How's your headache this morning?"

"Pretty good," Sandy said. She reached for her jeans. "I think aspirin will handle the problem today. That's a real blessing, because those prescription pills seem to make me too light-headed to concentrate the way I should."

Good, she was beginning to retain daily details, Wade thought. "Then you won't mind if I at least drive you to work."

"That's not necessary, honey. I can do it."

"It may not be necessary, but humor me, okay? I'll feel better knowing you got there safely."

"You're sweet." Sandy tugged on her jeans, one leg at a time, and wiggled them up her thighs till they were finally high enough to snap and zip. The hungry look of Wade's darkly compelling gaze made her smile. "Sorry."

"For what?"

"For getting you all excited when I have to leave," she said, approaching. "I'll make it up to you tonight when I get home, I promise."

Wade opened his mouth to argue, then changed his mind. There was no chance of fooling Sandy about his feelings when he couldn't even convince himself he didn't want to make love to her. Yes, it was a crazy idea, but that didn't mean he could turn off his physical reactions to a beautiful woman wearing nothing but formfitting jeans over high-cut panties and a lacy, white bra that showed the darker shadow of her nipples through the sheer fabric.

Sandy stopped mere inches from him and grinned more widely. "Thanks for laying my clothes out for me."

"You're welcome," he muttered, trying to ignore the sweet smell of her hair and the soft rise of her breasts above the skimpy lace. "You forgot to put on your blouse."

"Don't you want to kiss me first?"

Wade wondered if the legendary Hades was full of impossible temptations like this. It was a good bet it was, at least where men were concerned, he decided.

Leaning down, he placed a perfunctory kiss on her forehead. "There. Now, go get your shirt on and grab your purse. I'll make the toast you wanted and you can eat it while I drive."

"Okay, spoilsport," Sandy said with a mock sneer. "I'm going—I'm going."

Letting out his breath in a great whoosh as soon as she was back in the bedroom and out of sight, Wade sank against the doorjamb. *Egad,* was this nightmare never going to be over?

Heart pounding, he envisioned the moment when Sandy would regain her lost memory and once again leave him, and he wondered if this new parting was going to be as rough as the first time.

No, he decided easily. They were both older, more mature, more aware of their sexuality and the voids in their respective lives. Not only that, he could feel himself slipping, losing the rancor and bitterness he'd worked so hard to sustain. *Oh, no. This parting wasn't going to be as rough as before. It was going to be worse. Much worse.*

Wade handed Sandy a steaming coffee mug and a napkin for her buttered toast, then hustled her out the door to his truck. This time, he noted, she didn't question his ownership of the vehicle. In fact, she climbed into the cab as if she did it every day, laid her purse at her feet and placed her coffee mug in the drink holder on the center console so it wouldn't spill.

Noticing how closely Wade was watching her, she smiled over at him. "I'll be careful of your new toy, honey. I won't even get crumbs on the seat."

"Good." He started the engine and let it warm up for a minute. "Well, where to?"

"Rossmore Elementary," Sandy said, shooting him an incredulous gaze. "Poor Mrs. Lynch is probably going nuts without me."

Wade refrained from commenting and simply pulled out into traffic, heading for the familiar neighborhood campus. The doctor had told him Sandy might skip from one part of her life to another, but he hadn't mentioned that she might also return to a previously revisited era.

So far, he noted, everything she'd remembered, except for the events since her accident, had taken place before their separation and divorce. He supposed he shouldn't be surprised to learn she once again thought she was employed as an instructional aide, which explained why she hadn't complained about the casual clothing he'd laid out for her. Dresses and high heels were definitely not the proper attire for someone who had to spend hours on the playground looking after hundreds of rowdy kids every day.

Her obvious love of that particular job was one of the reasons he'd assumed Sandy would want children. She was so good with them. So patient. And they all seemed to love her in spite of the fact she had to make them behave when they would rather be running amok.

A sidelong glance told him she was not at all unsure about their destination, nor was she worried about being able to do her job once they arrived. As a matter of fact, she seemed quite content.

Almost to the school zone, Wade slowed the Dodge Ram to keep its speed within the limits of the law and wondered what he should do next. If he was going to tell Sandy she didn't really work there, he'd better do it soon, because they were almost out of time.

"Sandra?"

"Yes?"

Wade saw the joy in her expectant expression as she turned to look at him, and he decided he wasn't going to be the one to erase it this time. Let somebody else do the dirty deed. Him? He'd stand in the background and be ready to pick up the pieces after Sandy found out she was still confusing her past and present. That way she'd feel she had at least one friend left.

The group of one-story school buildings that made up the Rossmore campus loomed in the distance. Leafy green trees shaded the front lawn and gave the place a homey aura. Except for a recent paint job and some summer perennials planted in a narrow bed by the office, it looked exactly the way it had for as long as Wade could remember.

"Pull in there, behind the buses," Sandy said, pointing with one hand and dusting bread crumbs off her lap with the other. "You can let me out at the curb so you won't have to bother parking."

Wade shook his head. "I'll walk you in."

"Oh, come on," Sandy protested. "I'm not some kid who's been playing hooky." Fishing in her purse, she found a lipstick and quickly applied it, then smoothed her hair back with her hands.

"Just the same, I'm going to see you to the door," he insisted.

"Okay, okay. Suit yourself." She glanced at the small digital clock on the dash console. "Only hurry, will you? The first bell is about to ring."

After pulling into the nearest available space, Wade got out and circled the truck to open the door for Sandy. She was taking a last sip of coffee before climbing down and she looked so young, so exuberant, his heart bled for her. There was no telling how she would be received inside the school, and he began to wish he'd made some excuse to keep her home and spare her the trauma of learning that she wasn't who she thought she was.

Maybe this shock would help her get back to normal, though, he told himself, hoping to quiet his conscience. Maybe coming here and facing the truth was just the jolt she needed to finally recover.

And if it isn't? Wade followed Sandy through the front gate and onto the schoolyard, staying out of the way, yet keeping a close watch on her.

If the situation got out of hand when she tried to go to work at a job she hadn't held for three years or better, he'd be there for her and whisk her off before too much damage was done. It was all he could do short of locking her up till she came to her senses on her own.

A lump formed in his throat and he tensed all over. They'd know in a few minutes. She was going into the office.

"'Morning," Sandy said. "Where's Mary?"

A slim, taciturn woman behind the counter that divided the room into public and private areas peered out at her over the thin frames of her glasses and scowled. "I beg your pardon?"

"Mary. Oh, never mind. I can't stop to talk now. I'm late." Adroitly releasing the hidden catch on the swinging half door, Sandy hurried through the outer office and down the hall toward the employee lounge and workroom, thoroughly elated to be back in familiar territory.

Though she would have preferred to go straight to the classroom and explain her absence to the teacher she worked for, there was paperwork to take care of first. Personnel would have left an absence form in her private cubbyhole, otherwise known as a mailbox, and she'd have to fill that out and turn it in to the payroll clerk before she could technically go back to work.

Far-left row third box from the top had been hers ever since she'd started at the school and she knew its placement so well she didn't even have to look for her name on the lower front edge.

Shuffling through the assorted notices, half-done reports and personal items, she noticed her whistle hanging on its red-and-white braided lanyard, took it out and slipped it around her neck while she continued to search for the necessary absence form.

Someone tapped her on the shoulder. "Excuse me?"

Sandy glanced up for only a moment, noting a young, dark-haired woman dressed much the same as she was. "Hi. Sorry I can't stop to talk. I'm really late. You're new here, aren't you?"

"No."

"Well, I guess you and I just haven't run into each other yet. I work in first grade."

"You do?"

"Uh-huh." Scowling, Sandy straightened and readjusted the shoulder strap on her purse. "Darn. I can't seem to find my absence form. I guess Diane must have forgotten to give me one."

"Diane in the business office?"

"Sure. Who else?"

"Well, there's a Diane in the cafeteria and two teachers by that name, although one spells her name with an *A* on the end instead of an *E*."

Befuddled, Sandy ran her fingers through her hair. "I'm afraid I don't remember either of them."

"Maybe that explains why you're going through my mailbox," the other employee said.

"I am not!" Whirling, Sandy pushed back the messy pile of papers to expose the name tag at the base of the cubbyhole and prove her innocence. Her eyes widened. Instead of *Sandy Walker,* the label read *Rebecca Moore!*

Speechless, Sandy looked back at the girl, then returned her puzzled gaze to the stack of cubbyholes. How could she have made such a mistake? And if that was Rebecca's mailbox, then where was hers? Why had it been moved?

"I'm really sorry," Sandy said. "I'm used to having that one as mine, and I never stopped to look at the label."

Rebecca smiled and held out her hand. "That's okay. My whistle?"

"Oh, sure." Sandy slipped it off and gave it back. "I have one of my own in here somewhere."

"I'd help you look, but I have morning yard duty. Good luck," the dark-haired girl said with a parting wave.

Yeah, good luck, Sandy thought. She could use a little of that right now, especially since she was overdue in the classroom for before-school preparation and had yet to locate her absence form.

The receptionist approached slowly, as if wary of her. "Can I help you, ma'am?"

"Oh, no," Sandy said, throwing her hands in the air in frustration. "I just can't find my mailbox, that's all. Somebody must have rearranged them while I was sick."

"You were sick?" the woman asked.

"Uh-huh. But not for long. I can't understand..." She saw the woman focusing past her shoulder to the hallway behind her and a primitive shiver scurried up her spine. The passage, which was normally crowded with both teachers and support personnel in the mornings, was unusually quiet. Deserted. Except for one set of heavy footsteps Sandy heard approaching.

She turned, expecting to see a friendly face. Instead she was confronted by a burly, graying, security guard who was looking at her as though she were some sort of criminal.

"That's her," the receptionist squeaked. "She barged right in here as bold as you please and started going through the private boxes."

"I *work* here," Sandy insisted loudly, pointing her finger at the retreating woman. "She's the one who doesn't belong. Ask Mary. She'll tell you who I am."

The guard reached for Sandy's arm, but she eluded him by swinging her heavy purse between them. "No! Don't touch me. I belong here, I tell you. I work for Mrs. Lynch! *Everybody* knows me."

A small knot of curious adults had gathered in the doorway to the staff room. Desperate to prove her right to be there, Sandy scanned the tightly drawn faces. Of the seven, she recognized only two.

"Joan! Suzi! It's me. Tell them who I am," she called, fully expecting their prompt and friendly response. Neither of her old acquaintances moved or spoke.

Backing away, her hands raised in front of her to ward off the strangers closing in on her, Sandy headed for the front door. This misunderstanding was way too bizarre to deal with in the confines of the small office. Right now, all she could think of was getting out of there and finding somebody, anybody, who would confirm her identity.

She almost crashed into Wade as she bolted through the door onto the walkway. He stepped aside and let her pass because he could see other, more pressing, needs. Placing himself between the fleeing Sandy and the burly security guard who was following her, he blocked the man's way.

"I'll take care of this," Wade insisted. "She's just confused—she's not dangerous."

The stocky guard continued to try to bull his way past. "Just doin' my job, mister," he said. "Out of my way."

Firmly and with an unmistakable air of superior authority, Wade stood his ground, his aggressive stance and the insistent expression on his face holding sway. "I *said,* I'll take care of her."

The guard backed off a little, his hand resting on the two-way radio clipped to his belt. "Okay, okay, but I'll be right behind you. If she causes any more trouble, I'm calling the cops."

Wade's gaze followed Sandy down the hallway and past the school library. He knew just where she was going. The classroom she had originally worked in was located in that far block of buildings and she was obviously heading for the sanctuary of the only person she was still certain of; first-grade teacher Mrs. Lynch.

He started off at a fast trot, the guard hanging far enough behind to pose no immediate threat. Curious youngsters jumped out of his way and pointed, excited to see an adult breaking the strict school rules and racing down the sidewalk, when they themselves were forbidden from running in the halls.

Rounding the corner, Wade saw Sandy disappear into room seventeen and realized the guard was too far behind to have observed the same thing. "I think she got away," he shouted back. "You go that way, and I'll look over here."

To his great relief, the man did as he was told. Wade slowed to a walk and approached the squat, nondescript, classroom building. Rows of brightly colored plastic lunch boxes and discarded jackets were piled along the wall just outside each numbered door, waiting for their young owners to report for classes as soon as the morning bell rang.

Kids. The thought of happy children wrenched his stomach, making him glad he hadn't eaten any more breakfast than Sandy had.

Pausing, he stood at the closed door, his hand resting on the knob. *Well, better get this over with.* Taking a deep breath, he steeled his heart for whatever awaited him inside the empty classroom he'd seen Sandy duck into, tightened his grip and quietly eased open the door.

Chapter Ten

Sandy was standing in the middle of the room amid the scaled-down desks and weeping softly. A middle-aged woman with short, graying hair and the definite air of a capable, unruffled teacher was handing her tissues and muttering comforting platitudes.

"But it can't be," Sandy wailed. "I work for you. I do!"

Emma Lynch patted her on the back. "I'm sorry, dear. I wish I could tell you you're right, but that's not how it really is."

"It has to be!"

Mrs. Lynch glanced up at the black-rimmed wall clock over the chalkboard. "The bell will be ringing soon, and we can't have the children upset. Surely you understand that from the years when you *were* my aide."

"Of course. But if I don't belong here, then where do I belong?"

"With me," Wade said from the doorway. He nodded a greeting to the older woman. "We're sorry to have bothered you, ma'am. I'll take Sandra home now."

Obviously relieved, the teacher said, "Thank you," and turned her attention back to the stack of papers she had been distributing to each desk when interrupted.

Sandy felt a rush of intense gratitude for the timely rescue. "Oh, Wade..." She ran to him and fell into his arms as the heavy metal door closed behind her, leaving them alone outside in the bright sunshine. "It's all so frustrating! I'm beginning to think none of my life is real."

"It's real, honey. Too real, in some ways." Placing an arm around her shoulders in a protective embrace, he urged her toward the parking lot.

"Will you please explain it to me, then? This is getting really spooky." Sniffling, she dabbed at her eyes with the wad of tissues the teacher had given her.

"Only if your doctor says I should," he countered. "I'm not sure it would be for the best to go into detail at this point in time."

"For the *best?*" Stiffening, she stopped walking and scowled up at him through tear-filled eyes. "I'm going nuts here, Wade, and you're talking like it's up to you whether I learn the truth or not. Well, it isn't."

"Sorry you feel that way," he said, taking her arm to continue moving away from any place the security guard might be lurking. "But I figure you made it my business when you came to me for help."

"Well, maybe, but..." Sandy pulled her arm free of his hold but continued to walk alongside him. Scowling, she asked, "Did you know I wasn't employed at this school anymore when you brought me here?"

"Yes."

Wide-eyed, she stared up at him. "You did? And you let me come here anyway and make a complete fool of myself? Thanks a heap!"

"I didn't know what else to do."

"You could have tried the truth."

"Could I? I'm not too sure you can take hearing it."

"Suppose you let me be the judge of that." She realized that Wade was visibly concerned, yet her damaged pride kept needling her to press him for better, clearer answers. It was darned embarrassing to walk into a place where you were certain you belonged and find out everyone there thought you were demented!

They'd crossed the lawn and nearly reached the front gate just as a loud buzzer sounded. The last yellow-and-black bus in a long line was unloading its passengers. Children of all ages came running past them, book bags in hand, hair flying, shouting to each other.

A deep-seated habit surfaced and Sandy sang out, "Walk!" as if she actually were in charge of maintaining order. Acting on instinct, she reached for the stainless-steel whistle that no longer hung around her neck and her hand came up empty, further unnerving her.

"I *did* work here once, didn't I?" she asked, hoping Wade wasn't going to tell her she'd imagined that, too.

"Yes, you did. Only it was years ago."

"Years? Really?" The somber look in his eyes confirmed his statement better than any words could have. She stared down at her feet. "I see."

"Do you?"

Sandy managed a weak smile. "Actually, no. If you told me I'd been an astronaut in my spare time, or even run for president of the United States, I'd have to believe you. Apparently I've misplaced a few years of my life. Any idea how I can go about rediscovering them?"

"The doctor said it would all start to come back to you as soon as the swelling went down."

"Swelling? You mean up here?" She pushed the strap of her purse higher on her shoulder so she could probe her tender scalp with her fingertips. "I don't get it. I must have hit my head a dozen times in my life and I've never gotten amnesia before."

"It's not amnesia. It's called 'disorienting trauma,'" Wade informed her. "That's what's making you skip around and think you're in different years of your past, like high school, for instance."

"I what?" Pressing her hands to her forehead, Sandy closed her eyes and searched her recent memory. "The brownstone on Magnolia. I remember now. I tried to go see Jane Ellen, didn't I?"

"Yes."

"But she didn't live there anymore."

"Apparently not. You scared the dickens out of the present tenant, though."

"I don't doubt it." She took his hand and gave it a squeeze of gratitude. "As I recall, you were there to rescue me from that fiasco, too. Thanks."

"You're welcome."

Leaning her head against his shoulder, she momentarily closed her eyes and sighed. "So what do we do now?"

"That's up to you."

"Not a very comforting thought, is it? Especially since I don't seem to know what's what." She placed a weary kiss on the fabric of his shirt. "The only thing I am sure of is how exhausted I suddenly am."

"Then let's go home."

Sandy nodded in agreement. "*That* sounds like the best idea you've had this morning."

I will get better, she told herself over and over as she climbed into the black pickup and watched the man she loved slide behind the wheel. *And when I do, Wade and I will iron out whatever differences we may have had and get back to the normal life we used to lead.*

That thought gave her pause. *Differences? What differences?* As far as she could tell from watching him, he was accepting her illness as a matter of course and dealing with it calmly. They hadn't even had genuinely cross words that she could recall. So why was she getting the feeling they were at odds over something?

Sandy glanced over at him and was instantly overwhelmed by waves of love that flowed over and through her, leaving a familiar tingle from her toes all the way up to the knot on the top of her head. She might be injured and disoriented, but one thing was certain: she adored Wade Walker with every cell in her body and every thought in her soul. Even if the whole world as she knew it fell apart, that kind of pure passion was as everlasting as the universe.

It would never die.

The trip home was uneventful. Though she fully trusted Wade to look after her, Sandy still found herself wondering if what seemed to be happening to her at present was real or not. Once she had made herself admit she might be imagining things, the concept had undermined *all* her beliefs, leaving her unsure there was validity in any of her experiences.

One thing was sure, she decided almost immediately. From now on, she was going to go along with anything Wade suggested, even if she had to pretend she understood his reasoning, when she actually didn't have a clue. Then, when things started to make sense to her again, she'd be in a good position to make it all up to him.

Sandy smiled. Laying her head on his shoulder, she sighed. "So what do we do now?"

"I suppose I should take you to a doctor."

"We already did that."

"In a manner of speaking. I'm not sure the emergency clinic did an adequate job, though."

"Because I'm still confused?" she asked, knowing he would probably agree.

Wade nodded.

"Well, how long did they say it would take for me to be myself again?"

Glancing down at her, he shook his head and smiled. "You know, the problem you've been having must be contagious, because I honestly can't remember. A few days, I think."

"Seems like I do recall the doctor telling me to take it easy and not worry till Monday. That gives us the rest of this week." Sandy paused, her hands tightening on his upper arm as he drove. "Will you promise me one thing, Wade?"

"If I can."

"I want you to swear you'll tell me the truth about my life from now on so I don't get into more trouble the way I did this morning."

"For instance?" He held his breath, praying she wouldn't ask about the underlying reasons for their divorce, then remembered she didn't even know they'd gotten one.

"Well . . . like my clothes. Where are they?"

"In your apartment, I assume," he said. "I'd already decided I should take you there pretty soon so you could pick up a few things you might need."

Sandy forced herself to appear calmly unconcerned. "Of course. My apartment. Why didn't I think of that?"

"You remember it?" Now he was truly encouraged. If she was that far along in her rehabilitation, it shouldn't be long till she was completely cured.

"I have this vague picture of the place," Sandy fibbed. "Can you find the way without my help?"

"I think so." He reached into his pants pocket and got her driver's license with the address.

Pulling away from him, she scowled. "*You* took it out of my purse? Why?"

"To protect you," he said. "I was afraid that if you saw it before you were ready to accept the changes in your life and trust me implicitly, you'd panic and try to run away."

"Why on earth would I do that?"

Wade shrugged and smiled. "Well, between the screaming, the crying and the giggles, you did seem to be a fraction unbalanced. It was hard to tell what to expect."

"And the kisses," she said softly. "Don't forget those."

"I'm not likely to."

"Good." Sandy saw him gripping the wheel, his knuckles whitening beneath his healthy tan. Whatever was responsible for her husband's current aversion to sex, it seemed to be the only constant in their relationship. *Terrific.*

Closing her eyes for a few seconds in order to shut out all distractions, she tried to imagine any instances prior to her bicycle accident when Wade had refused to make love to her. As far as she could tell, there weren't any. That, however, was no criterion, since she apparently didn't even know where she lived!

Sandy blinked rapidly and cleared her vision. Unfortunately her brain remained clouded.

She sat back and waited. It was beginning to seem as if everything she said or did annoyed him. Which was crazy, considering their congenial marriage.

Sandy's first reaction was to return the same degree of ire he was exhibiting, but she stifled the urge. Until she was fully back to her old self, there was no guarantee that her past with Wade was anything like the way she remembered it, so how could she blame him for reactions she couldn't explain?

Could their life have been sad? she wondered for the first time. The thought gave her the shivers and raised goose bumps on her arms. Of all the possibilities, that was the most frightening.

He tossed the plastic folder containing her California driver's license and personal photos onto her lap. "There. That's who you are and where you live."

"It is?" Sandy gingerly lifted the shiny plastic window and stared at the unflattering photo of herself. Her hair had been really short when the picture was taken and she'd been wearing large, dangling hoop earrings, the kind she knew Wade disliked.

"This is me?" When he shot her a funny look, she quickly amended her statement. "I mean, of course this is me. It looks just the way I'm supposed to. The address sounds very familiar, too."

"That's great. There's a Riverside County map in the console. Get it out and look up Glenwood Street for me, will you? I think we're close."

"Sure." Sandy scooted over to make room for the center console to fold down between them and opened it, taking out the local map. If this was Wade's not-so-subtle way of getting her to sit all the way across the truck, he'd have to do better than that, especially if he hoped to keep her there.

She peered at the fine print on the map, her finger tracing streets till she found what she was searching for. "It looks like you turn south on Market and follow it all the way to the end, then veer left."

"Got it."

Studying the map further, she felt a strange sense of déjà vu, as if she really did recognize some of the street names and locations.

Which is perfectly normal, she insisted. *All I have to do is concentrate and I'll be fine.*

She focused intensely. Names and places began darting into her conscious mind, only to vanish like a puff of smoke on a windy day before she could identify them clearly. The harder she tried to remember details or place them in any usable order, the more scattered and tenuous her thoughts became. Finally she had to give up entirely and lay the map aside.

Relax, she told herself, taking deep breaths and trying to let them out slowly so Wade wouldn't realize how upset she was getting. *It will come. Just give it time.*

Glancing sidelong at Wade, she found herself wondering if she was the only one confused in their family. After all, she had only his word that her head injury had caused such severe memory loss.

Except for what happened at school this morning, she added with a scowl. There was certainly no way he could have influenced all those people to doubt her, was there?

And why would he want to? Sandy turned her head to boldly study him.

"What's wrong?" Wade took his eyes off the road long enough to cast her a questioning look.

"Nothing."

"Then why are you staring at me?"

"Sorry," she said, gazing out the window and seeing nothing. "I was just thinking."

"About us?" He tensed all over. Maybe it was finally the right time to tell her their marriage had been legally dissolved. He certainly hoped so. He was getting darned sick of having to avoid the truth and coddle Sandy while his own emotions ground his gut to ribbons. If he didn't have an ulcer before, he sure as hell was working on one now.

"No," she said, "about you."

"Oh." Chagrined, Wade decided to hold his peace and let her ramble on for the present, since that was what she seemed to want to do. "Okay. What about me?"

"I . . . I don't know quite how to say this."

"Just spit it out. You won't hurt my feelings."

Pressing her lips into a thin line, she took a moment to organize her perceptions, then began. "I think it may be possible you're trying to convince me I'm more confused than I really am."

"I'm what?"

"Don't go getting mad, okay? It was just a thought and you said you could take hearing it."

Wade forced himself to calm down, at least where it showed. "You're right. I did say that. I'm sorry I snapped at you." He stared at the narrowing street ahead and continued to drive toward the address on Glenwood. "Do you have any inkling why I might want to mess with your mind?"

"No. Not really. I do think it has something to do with our marriage, though."

"For instance?"

Sandy shook her head in frustration and worry. "For instance, if I had a separate apartment all along, why didn't you mention it when I first came to you?"

"You were too sick. All I could think about was taking proper care of you."

"Was I? And what about later? I'm not in much pain anymore, yet you conveniently failed to inform me I'd be walking into trouble if I went to Rossmore this morning. Why was that, Wade?"

He stiffened. "Hell, I don't know. I thought about telling you, but you weren't acting like you'd be likely to believe me anyway. You seemed so determined and positive about your job I decided to let you find out the truth for yourself. I was hoping the shock would bring you back to normal."

"Which is?"

"I beg your pardon."

"What's normal for me, Wade? Who am I and what am I, if I'm not who I think I am?"

"You sure you want to hear this?"

Sandy was getting genuinely upset. "*Yes*, I'm sure. Do you think I enjoy running around town making a fool of myself and wondering if anything I experience is real?" She paused to look out the window as he pulled the pickup to the curb. "Why are you stopping?"

"Because this is where you live," he said, his jaw muscles clenching. "I think we should go inside if we're going to have a serious talk."

The momentary sight of the modern, triple-story, neutral-beige apartment complex gave Sandy a jolt. There *was* something vaguely familiar about the place, although she couldn't tell exactly what aspects of the building and its grounds made her feel that way.

"Do you have a key with you or shall I go find the manager to let us in?" Wade asked.

"I...I'm sure I have a key." Rooting through her bag, she located a ring of keys, several of which looked as if they would fit a front door. Rather than admit she had no idea which one to use, she handed the entire bunch to Wade without comment.

"Good. Come on," he said, climbing down and circling around to her side of the truck.

Sandy was already standing beside the vehicle when he got to her. Trembling, in spite of the warm temperature and bright, springtime sun, she folded her arms across her chest to still the shivers. "You go first."

"Okay. Whatever you say."

As she watched him walking away from her, a sudden sense of impending loss wrapped around her like an ominous, gray thundercloud. Something was wrong. Seriously wrong. And she was certain the revelation of whatever it was could be found inside the apartment they were about to visit.

She hung back, unwilling to face the unknown.

Noticing that she was no longer with him, Wade paused and turned. "You coming?"

"I don't know."

"Why?"

Sandy felt a cold chill run up her spine and settle in her heart, where it was made welcome. "For some reason, I don't like this place."

"Nonsense." Wade retraced his steps, took her by the hand and led her along the cement walkway to the base of the wrought-iron exterior stairs that led to the upper floors.

"You're in number two-eleven, so it has to be up here. Come on."

Sandy paused to get her breath and gather her courage. There was profound sadness associated with this place; she could feel it all the way to her bones. Yet she also sensed that she did truly belong here. If that was the case, then what about her idyllic married life? Was it a dream or reality?

Feeling the same unreasonable fear of abandonment she remembered so vividly from her childhood, she forced herself to face it and begin to climb the open staircase behind Wade.

Even if it meant more grief, more senseless tears, she had to validate her life so she could start looking forward to the future instead of floundering in a morass of past memories.

Chapter Eleven

Wade only had to try two keys before he found the right one. Opening the door slowly, he looked inside. Without a doubt, this was Sandy's home.

The living room had a soft, feminine charm, yet it wasn't frilly or uncomfortable looking the way a lot of places were. She'd kept the velvet-flowered, bluish gray couch they'd had in their den, he noted, as well as the matching, marble-based lamps they'd picked out together one blissful afternoon just prior to their garden wedding.

He guessed that shouldn't have surprised him, but it did. Not that he'd thrown out all the furniture tied to his memories of Sandy, either, it was just odd to open the door to a strange apartment and suddenly feel so at home. Stepping aside, he made room for her to enter.

Sandy glanced at him as she passed, her eyes pleading for help and forbearance. There was no doubt in her mind she had at least a nodding acquaintance with this place, since she did recognize some of the furniture. The walls seemed the wrong shade of off-white, though, and the striped wallpaper behind the sofa was definitely not something she had put there.

Taking a few more tentative steps, she looked at the plush, beige carpeting beneath her feet, where she knew there should be hardwood floors, instead. The end tables were wrong, too. The lamps were hers, but someone must have somehow substituted different tables.

A sudden flash of remembrance confounded her, its message clear, its strength overwhelming. Sandy froze, gathering her random thoughts into a coherent package. Not only did she know what she needed to do, she was certain she knew exactly how to accomplish it!

Spurred on by her cohesive thoughts, she acted immediately, sprinting from the living room and down a short hallway. The first door she came to was the bathroom; the second, the bedroom. Ignoring everything but the precious photo she was looking for, she hurried to the dresser and snatched up the silver frame she knew would be atop it.

Wade followed. Concerned, he approached to question her. "What happened? Did you remember something?"

"Yes," Sandy said, hugging the picture frame to her chest, face in. "I don't know why, but I knew this was here and I had to be sure it was still okay."

"What is it?"

"Our wedding picture," she said, gazing up at him with eyes of pure love.

"You keep it on display in your bedroom?"

"Of course I do." Sandy continued to clutch the photograph as she slowly looked around the strange room. There were plain, white blinds on the windows instead of the sheers and drapes she preferred, and the bed was too narrow for two people to sleep comfortably, although the headboard did match the maple dresser and mirror frame.

"Except, this isn't my room," she said after a moment's perusal. "It can't be. I've never been here before."

"Then how did you know about the picture you're holding?" Since she had obviously remembered one pertinent detail in an instant, Wade couldn't help hoping she'd regain more of her lost memory the same way.

"I don't know. Maybe I guessed."

"And went straight to the bedroom without ever having been here before? Not likely."

"Then you tell me," Sandy snapped. "You're the so-called expert on me and my life. *You* figure it out."

Taken aback by her hostile response, he decided to hold off making any other specific observances till he was sure she would be able to accept them. In the meantime, there was a chance she might make more positive progress by merely going through the motions of gathering up the clothing and personal items they had come there for in the first place.

Calm and unruffled, at least on the outside, Wade leaned nonchalantly against the open doorway. "Settle down, honey. I didn't bring you here so we could fight. All I want is for you to pick up some clothes and whatever other stuff you need so we can take it back to my place and make you more comfortable while you're staying with me."

"While I'm *what?*" His blasé attitude was definitely getting under her skin and she saw no reason to continue hiding her consternation.

"You're staying with me," Wade said slowly. "You live here and I live in the old house we used to share."

"I do not!"

He shook his head sadly. "Yes, you do."

"Prove it." Sandy was not about to accept a concept so foreign to her. She'd all but forgotten her decision to fake normalcy and was totally caught up in fighting the suggestion that she and her husband were no longer living together.

"How?" He swept his arm in a wide arc. "I can't very well notify your neighbors you were hurt and get them to assure you, because if they know you're not going to be home for a while, one of them might decide to burglarize your place while you're gone.''

"They would never do a thing like that.''

"How do you know? If you don't remember living here, then how can you vouch for the integrity of the other tenants?''

Sandy's head was beginning to pound. She sank onto the edge of the bed, one hand on her forehead, and laid the photo aside on the pale, rose-patterned spread. "I don't know.''

Sorry to see her suffering so, Wade sat down beside her and took her hand. "Look, Sandy. I know it may not seem like it sometimes, but I really am trying to help you.''

"Then tell me what's going on? Why do we live apart and why don't I remember anything about it?''

Tears were gathering in her eyes, making him wish there was something he could say that would make the world into the pretty place she wanted it to be. Only there wasn't. The lovely universe of their youthful dreams was long gone and with it their marriage.

Finally he decided it was time to break the harsh news to her in spite of his heart's arguments against doing so.

"I don't know why you can't remember anything about that part of our past,'' he said, trying to be comforting while at the same time delivering the coup de grace. "But you live away from me because that's the way it's supposed to be when two people are divorced.''

Astonishment temporarily paralyzed Sandy. Shouting "No!'' she broke the awful spell and jumped to her feet. The sudden rush of blood away from her brain made her dizzy, only to be followed a few seconds later by the return of the intense cranial pressure attributable to her head injury.

Reeling, she staggered backward, away from the man who had promised to remain her husband forever. Flashes of light and brilliant-colored spheres appeared behind her eyes to further obscure her already cloudy vision. At the edges of her mind, darkness waited, beckoning her into its quietude and peace.

She saw Wade rise and start toward her, seeming to move in slow motion, while his ugly words pounded through her mind, leaving new pain and anguish wherever they touched. It wasn't right. It wasn't fair. They couldn't be divorced. She'd vowed to be his for the rest of her life and that was how it was always supposed to be!

The blackness increased, folding in, soothing her torment, quickly leaving only a single point of light. In it, she saw Wade's darkly compelling gaze reflecting the bitter truth: they were no longer wed.

Closing her eyes against a reality she refused to accept, Sandy stopped fighting to remain aware, crumpled and slid toward the floor, her mind eager for the perfect rest and escape unconsciousness promised.

Wade saw her start to collapse and was at her side in an instant, bearing her up in his arms and carrying her a few steps to the bed. Standing there, holding the woman he had once loved with all his heart in his arms, he decided against putting her down where they were and turned instead toward the living room, laying her gently on the sofa.

He'd had quite enough of romantic encounters in bedrooms, he told himself. It was bad enough he and Sandy had to live in the same house while she recovered, let alone occupy the same bed. When all this nonsense was over, he swore he'd never complain about sleeping alone again.

Sandy began to stir. Opening her eyes, she saw Wade bending over her, his expression one of concern in spite of the news he had so callously delivered.

Licking her lips first, she whispered, "Divorced?"

"Yes." He straightened.

"How long?"

"Two years."

"I don't believe you."

"I can't help that. It's true," he said soberly.

She raised up on one elbow and fingered the small, opal ring she always wore on the third finger of her left hand. "Then why am I still wearing your ring?"

"I wondered that myself," Wade said, making his way to the foot of the couch so he couldn't easily reach down and touch her the way he wanted to. "I guess you just like opals. After all, it doesn't look much like the customary gold band, does it?"

Sandy couldn't argue that point. Swinging her feet to the floor, she sat up rapidly and momentarily swayed.

Wade was by her side immediately, steadying her shoulders till she looked stable, then quickly letting her go. "Take it slow, will you? I'm getting tired of picking you up off the floor."

"Sorry." She rubbed her stinging eyes and shook her head in disbelief. "Tell me again. We really aren't married anymore?"

"Nope."

"What happened?"

Now, there was a question and a half, he thought, determined to keep the sordid details of their alienation to himself. Sandy had keeled over when he simply mentioned divorce. No telling what the rest of the story would do to her. Wade wasn't about to start explaining and find out the hard way.

"It doesn't matter," he said flatly. "It's all over and done with. Forget it. I have."

"Forget it?" Her eyes widened, filling with unshed tears. "Just like that, forget all the love and happiness we had together? How can you suggest such a thing?"

"It's easier after a couple of years," he said, pacing away from her across the small living room. "Art will tell you. I had my bad days, but I got through them. So did you. All you have to do is try to remember adjusting to single life the first time so you don't have to struggle through it all over again."

"Terrific." Cynicism was beginning to fill Sandy's troubled thoughts as her mind probed its hidden depths in a supreme effort to recall her split from Wade and the subsequent dissolution of the idyllic marriage she had been convinced would last for eternity.

He snorted with derision. "Yeah. Tell me about it. I was fine till you showed up on my doorstep a couple of days ago and brought it all back to me. It hasn't been easy looking after you." *And not making passionate love to you in the process,* he added silently.

Sandy was beginning to feel decidedly unwanted and unwelcome negative emotions she didn't relish one bit. "Fine," she said firmly. "Then don't do it anymore. Go home and leave me alone."

"I can't."

"Sure you can. I live here, right?"

Scowling, he regarded her cautiously when he said, "Yes."

"Then this is where I intend to stay."

"Not alone, you don't."

"Who says?"

Wade glared at her. "*I* do. You weren't even sure what your name was, day before yesterday. What if you revert to that degree of confusion and wander off? What then?"

"Then you can print my picture on a milk carton and make me infamous, for all I care," she countered. "It's obvious you don't want anything more to do with me, so I release you from any stupid promises you may have made. Go away, Wade. Let me alone."

The stubborn look on his face said "Make me" more clearly than any words could have. Folding his arms across his broad chest, he widened his already formidable stance and stood like an ancient warrior ready to do battle.

As determined as he, Sandy faced up to him boldly. "If you don't get out of here, I swear I'll call the police."

"And tell them what?" He sneered, mimicking female speech as he said, "Help me, Officer. I think I may live here and this guy looks familiar, but I have no idea where I work or anything else about myself." His deep, resonant voice returned to normal. "Try it. I dare you. They'll lock you up and throw away the key."

Like it or not, Sandy had to admit he was right. The advantage she had, though, was the apartment itself. Surely it held answers to many of her questions, if not all of them. An examination of the premises was the first thing she must do.

That decided, she wondered how she'd convince Wade she was well enough to conduct her search without him peering over her shoulder and interfering with what tenuous privacy she had left. Sandy made a low sound of disgust. *Couldn't be much harder than compiling actuary tables from scratch,* she thought, wondering immediately where she'd gotten such an obscure comparison.

Wade had been watching her and was quick to spot the look of bewilderment in her eyes. "What is it? What else do you remember?"

"Nothing, I guess," Sandy said, slowly shaking her head. She glanced around the room, her gaze coming to rest on the telephone table with a shallow drawer beneath. "I don't care what you do, but I'm going to stay right here and look this place over."

"That's the first sensible thing you've said in a long time," he agreed. "Poke around. Maybe you'll see something that brings it all back to you and we can be done with each other for good."

She bristled. "For a man who claims he's anxious to dump me, you sure are hard to get rid of. Why is that?" Crossing to the small table, she pulled open the drawer and began paging through the personal address book she found there. When Wade didn't answer, she looked back at him and added, "Well?"

"Damned if I know," he grumbled. "Maybe I'm as crazy as you are."

Sandy smiled. "Now you're talking."

An up-to-date calendar was posted on the inside of one of the kitchen-cabinet doors. From the look of the precise, day-by-day notations, including the vacation time she was currently spending, Sandy had to assume she was one of those people who wrote everything down because she had a habit of forgetting details.

Of course, that was true only if the apartment was really hers. Which it had to be, she admitted ruefully. Whatever faults Wade might have, cruel subterfuge was not one of them.

She glanced over at him and immediately wished she hadn't. His hair was mussed just enough to give him a rakish air, his shirt was open at the collar, revealing a smattering of the curly, dark hair that graced the rest of his chest, and his chin was beginning to show a shadow of whiskers, which emphasized the strong planes of his face. All in all, he looked too darned appealing to suit her.

He'd taken up residence on a tall kitchen stool and was leaning on the elevated countertop, thumbing through her address book to see if he knew any of the people she couldn't identify. Not that his personal input actually mattered, Sandy confessed. Searching through the tattered little book was simply an assignment she had given him to keep him out of her hair while she explored.

Easing toward the door, she was disappointed when he looked up and warned, "Don't go far."

"I thought you were busy," she countered.

"I am. But I'm never too absorbed to notice what you're up to."

"Great." Sandy made a pouting face. "I hope you're not going to insist you go with me from room to room just because I get a little faint once in a while."

"Not as long as you promise me you won't fall on your face again."

"I'll try not to."

"Good." Wade put aside the small address book and gazed at her soberly. "If you're interested, which you should be, I think I've got your dizzy spells figured out."

"Go on."

"They seem to occur whenever your headaches are the worst and you make a quick movement. Chances are, the fainting has something to do with pressure in your head, same as the original injury."

"You think so?"

"Yes, especially because I never knew you to faint in the past."

She paused and regarded him seriously. "You know, you may be right."

"Probably." Wade knew he appeared more smug and pleased with himself than the moment warranted, but he couldn't help feeling elated. Sandy had always been unreasonably stubborn and hardheaded, even when they were madly in love. To hear her actually admit he was correct about a problem she had failed to figure out did his ego so much good he almost forgot why they were there.

"Okay. I'll go at it slowly and try not to get mad."

"That sounds like a good start." He made a move to stand, clearly intending to follow her into the next room.

Sandy held up one hand like a traffic cop on duty at a busy corner. "Stop where you are. I want to look over the personal items in the bedroom and bathroom by myself."

"But..."

"No," she insisted. "You stay there and let me do this alone. My head is feeling a lot better and I'm sure I won't faint again."

"Famous last words."

She placed her hands on her hips and faced him with determination. "Last words? That isn't funny, Wade."

"It wasn't meant to be."

The spunky pose Sandy had assumed reminded him of when they were dating. So did her svelte figure beneath her clothing, which his agile mind quickly removed, leaving her as bare as she'd been when she'd gotten dressed in front of him that morning.

Visualizing her as a beautiful, naked goddess, boldly challenging him with the fire of glistening gold and emeralds in her eyes, did funny things to Wade's composure, things he couldn't completely hide.

Sandy scowled over at him. "What's the matter?"

"Nothing."

"Oh, sure. I thought you were going to be honest with me. That's what you said."

"This has nothing to do with honesty, Sandra."

"Then what is it about? You have a pretty peculiar look on your face."

"I do not."

"Hah! Want me to get you a mirror?"

Wade didn't have to look at his reflection to know exactly what was manifested in his telling expression. It was lust; pure, unadulterated lust. And it embarrassed him deeply to admit it, even to himself. Confessing to Sandy was totally out of the question.

"Just go do whatever it was you wanted to do," Wade said gruffly. "I'll wait here."

"You will?" She was clearly surprised, yet withheld full acceptance of his promise till she'd asked, "Why?"

"Because you told me to."

That did it. Sandy crossed the room and leaned on the opposite side of the counter, going nose to nose with him. "I may have forgotten a lot of things, Wade Walker, but I know you never gave in to me that easily before, so what's going on? Are you trying to get rid of me because you want to search the rest of my apartment yourself, or have you found somebody in the address book I should call?''

He shook his head, his jaw muscles clenching. Didn't she know what she was doing to him? Couldn't she tell? They'd been enthusiastic lovers for months once. Surely that part of their life together hadn't left her consciousness altogether.

The sweet, fresh smell of her hair teased his senses and left him breathless. Looking into her eyes, Wade willed her to understand the danger, to flee before it was too late, to go back across the room and leave him alone to drown in the misery of his unfulfilled yearning.

He saw carnal knowledge dawn in her eyes, softening her insistent pose and causing her to lean ever so slightly toward him, her lips parting as she moved closer.

''Wade . . .''

''Don't,'' he warned, his voice husky with desire. ''Don't say a word and don't be nice to me if you know what's good for you. I'm right on the verge of grabbing you and carrying you off to the bedroom.''

''I know,'' Sandy whispered. ''What I don't understand is why you haven't done it before.''

Chapter Twelve

Time ceased to pass. Sandy was certain the thundering beating of her heart could be heard in adjoining apartments, if not all the way to the street.

If she leaned closer, would Wade kiss her, or would he run from the erotic pleasures she was offering the way he had before? Dared she take a chance? Licking her lips, she waited and wondered, praying he'd finally sweep her up in his strong arms and make her his, the way fate had ordained.

She could see the subtle changes in his expression. Perspiration began to bead on his forehead, yet he remained as still as granite. Why was he fighting so hard to resist, when she could see desire represented so plainly on his handsome face? Wade was not a man to turn away from love. At least, he never had been when they were a couple. So what was stopping him now?

The moment she whispered ''Wade...?'' her voice filled with pure passion, he seemed to gain strength rather than lose ground. She saw his jaw set with firm resolve.

The idea that his resistance to their making love had to have been brought on by some catastrophic occurrence came to her in an unexpected flash of divine insight, taking her breath away. But *what?* What could have happened that was so bad he was unwilling to forgive?

Reaching out with trepidation, Sandy touched his hand. "Tell me, Wade. What came between us?"

He pulled away, the spell broken, and got to his feet. "I already told you—it doesn't matter. Now, drop it, Sandra."

"But that's not being fair. How can I hope to patch things up between us if you won't tell me what went wrong in the first place."

"Humph." He shot her a frigid glance. "I'm sure you'll remember soon enough. When you do, don't come running to me with any more lame excuses. I've heard them all and there's no way you'll ever get me to change my mind. Got that?"

The vehemence in his reply cut her to the soul. This was a side of Wade's personality she didn't recognize and was not prepared to accept, no matter what his reasons for such unjustifiable behavior.

Her first, gut-level impulse was to cry, but she quickly replaced it with a more productive response. Once, when they were younger, she might have crumpled like a fallen leaf under his relentless onslaught. Now, however, she looked deeply into her grieving heart and found more latent strength available than she'd imagined.

"Yes," Sandy said, standing tall and straight, her chin thrust out with determination, "I've got it. I may not have the details, but I certainly get your drift. I take it the divorce was your idea."

"It was mutual," he countered dryly.

"I see. And you have no intention of telling me what happened to turn you against me, do you?"

"No. None."

"Then that's the way it will have to be." There was deeply felt cynicism in her voice and facial expression. "I'm going into the bedroom to look around and I expect you to either stay where you are or get out of my house. Clear?"

"Very."

"Good. Maybe if we're both lucky I'll turn up something useful and regain my memory so you can disappear from my life the way you want to." She turned abruptly and started for the door. "At least I hope so."

Wade was ready to say "Me, too," but his mouth refused to form the words. To him, this whole experience was like a nightmare with soft, velvet edges, a horrible snare guarded by a beautiful, fallen angel.

She was probably thinking she'd cheated on him with another man, Wade mused. He sighed, wishing her sin had been such a simple one. But no. Sandy had been faithful, at least where their marriage bed was concerned, yet there were other ways to break faith with someone, weren't there? Other, more insidious ways to shake one person's belief in another.

The lying. The lame excuses. The loss. That was what he could never forget. He had trusted her with his life, his future, and she had betrayed that trust, leaving him bereft and alone. He had sworn then never to open his heart to any woman again and he hadn't. Till now.

Wade turned to gaze, unseeing, out the kitchen window and hide his emotional response to the unsettling thoughts while he struggled to compose himself. Cursing quietly, he had to admit Sandy had gotten to him with her innocent behavior and the tortured look in those sparkling, green eyes of hers.

Maybe he should have taken her up on her offer to make love while she was still willing, he reasoned, because once she did remember what had happened and all the anguish it had caused, he was certain she wouldn't let him within ten miles of her, let alone invite him into her bed.

Entering the master suite, Sandy took the time to look around more fully than she had when she'd barged in there to retrieve her wedding picture. The place was starting to feel vaguely familiar, although that might be due to no more than the fact she'd been in the room a few minutes before.

She paused, hands on her hips. It was hard enough to think straight when her head hurt. Quarreling with Wade had added another dimension to her agitated mental state and she wondered whether she'd ever be able to concentrate enough to unravel the secrets of her life.

"Of course I will," she told herself aloud, only half believing it. Probing gently, she touched the bump on her scalp and discovered that the swelling had gone down appreciably. That *was* good news! It not only meant she would soon be back to normal, it was proof the doctor at the clinic had known what he was talking about and she could quit worrying about her eventual recovery.

Comforted, Sandy walked slowly across the room. The bed was not unusual, nor was the dresser. However, off to one side was a small, maple writing desk she had overlooked until now. Hair prickled on the back of her neck. If it contained bills or other personal papers, it could be extremely valuable in her quest for answers.

The desk was the kind where the writing surface folds up to save space. Lowering the front, she opened it fully to reveal an answering machine with its digital readout listing two calls! Her heart pounded. This was more like it!

Hands shaking, she reached out to push the button that said Play. By the third word, she knew who her caller was.

"Hi, Sandy. It's me. You didn't call when you got back from the mountains like you said you would so I thought I'd check up on you. Call me when you can. Bye."

Jane! That was Jane Ellen! It had to be. But she hadn't left a number. *Darn!* Sandy had already double-checked her address book, finding no reference to her old friend at all.

Still thinking about Jane, she heard the machine playing the second message. It was from her mother and simply added to the consternation she'd felt when they'd last seen each other at Wade's.

Sandy replayed the message from her old friend twice more, listening to the pleasant voice and racking her brain for the phone number she had evidently failed to jot down because it was committed to memory.

Discouraged, she absently leafed through the unpaid bills stacked in one cubbyhole of the petite desk. All of them were addressed to her, leaving no lingering doubt that the apartment was truly hers.

"So, now what?" she muttered. If she stayed there, among the manifestations of the life she had obviously made for herself after her divorce, how could she be sure the necessary details of her past would ever come back to her? This was a separate existence. A totally new life. Even if she did manage to eventually function normally without really remembering everything, would there always be a chasm of lost knowledge to deal with, to wonder and agonize about?

And what should she do about Wade? she asked herself. It was clear he had suffered terribly, yet there was still enough mutual attraction between them to ignite the very air every time they looked at each other. And when they touched!

A shiver of anticipation skittered up Sandy's spine. It wasn't fair to either of them to simply walk away, when their relationship held such marvelous potential. So they'd had some serious differences. So what? With such a strong affinity for each other, surely there was a chance she could rebuild their broken partnership into at least a semblance of the warm friendship they had once shared.

Taking a deep breath to reinforce her courage, Sandy closed the desk, turned and made her way back to Wade, more than a little surprised to find him exactly where she had left him.

"I've decided something," she said before she could change her mind.

He looked up, his brows furrowing. "What?"

"I'm going home with you after all." She smiled at the comical expression of aversion that crossed his face. "I knew you'd be pleased."

"Oh, sure." Wade folded and laid aside the week-old newspaper he'd been perusing to pass the time. "What made you decide to do that? Have you remembered enough to make you want to torture me or something?"

"Not hardly. I just think I'll be more likely to fill in the missing years of my life if I start at the point I do recall, rather than staying here, where I'm even more confused."

"Did you find anything useful in the bedroom?"

"Only an answering machine."

"And?" Looking encouraged, Wade got to his feet.

"Jane Ellen had called. Unfortunately she neglected to leave her number. I assume I'm supposed to know it by heart."

Wade hefted the address book in the palm of his hand as if testing it for weight. "It's also possible she's married and you have her listed under her husband's name."

The idea gave Sandy a flutter of hope. "You think so?"

"I don't know. You could start at the beginning and call everybody till you find out one way or the other."

"I could, couldn't I!"

"Yes. And I think using your own telephone is the best choice, don't you?"

Seeing what he was up to, Sandy began to grin. "Not really. It could take the rest of the day or longer to make all those calls and it would be better if I were in familiar surroundings so that I'm that much closer to regaining all my memory."

Stuffing his hands into his pockets, Wade considered her suggestion. "You're really serious about this?"

"Completely. Since you refuse to tell me what it is I seem to have buried in my subconscious, then the only opportunity left to me is to either remember on my own or reach Jane Ellen in the hope that she will be able to help." Pausing, Sandy smiled over at him. "Besides, if I do manage to locate her, maybe she'll take me off your hands."

"Now you're beginning to make sense," Wade said. "All right. Go get some clothes packed and meet me at the truck." He held up the address book. "I'll take care of this for you."

"Okay." Her smile fading, Sandy watched him go. The easiest thing to do would be to remain in her cozy little apartment and rest till her head injury healed, thereby avoiding any chance of conflict or sorrow. The trouble was, making that choice would mean she would be giving up the opportunity to spend a few more precious hours or days with Wade and that wasn't an equitable trade-off. Even in her bewildered state, she knew that her husband's nearness, his comforting touch, was all that truly mattered.

Except Wade isn't my husband anymore, she told herself, not wanting to believe such an impossible premise. Yet it was true. The part of her heart that had resisted acceptance of Wade's veracity was now ready to capitulate in spite of her personal feelings and arguments to the contrary.

They were divorced. She knew it. And within the cloudy memory was a deeper, more poignant secret, lingering just out of reach no matter how hard she tried to retrieve it.

The answers to all her questions lay in the house they had once shared, Sandy thought, beginning to throw random pieces of clothing into a pile on the bed. She didn't care how long she had to stay at Wade's or what awful secrets she had to deal with. Any sacrifice would be worth bearing for the sake of the eternal love they had somehow lost. Even in her confused state, Sandy knew that was true, without a doubt.

Wade had spent the past fifteen minutes calling himself every kind of fool for agreeing to take Sandy back to his place when his feelings for her were so strong. By the time she made her way toward the truck, he had rationalized enough to convince himself he was only doing it to be rid of her sooner.

He took the lightweight suitcase from her and stowed it in the extra cargo space behind the Dodge Ram's seat. ''Did you lock up?''

''Yes.'' She glanced back at the upstairs apartment, feeling only a small tug of remembrance.

''I'm glad you found a suitcase. I wondered if you had one.''

Pausing, Sandy chewed thoughtfully on her lower lip. ''I don't know how I knew it was stored in the hall closet. I just needed it and went straight to it.''

''That's good,'' Wade said, helping her into the truck. ''It means you're closer to a cure.''

''I hope so.'' She sighed. ''It's good of you to let me come home with you.''

He chuckled wryly and shook his head. ''It's not like you gave me a whole lot of choice.''

''You're a big boy,'' Sandy countered. ''If you didn't want me for a houseguest all you had to do was say so.''

''Did I?'' Looking over at her, he started the engine. ''Seems to me you didn't leave me much room to argue.'' His countenance darkened. ''Which is not unusual, for you.''

''Really? I sort of had the impression we used to do things your way most of the time.''

Wade let out a guttural sound of contempt. ''Not when it counted.''

Unable to come up with a clever retort in the face of his evident displeasure, Sandy kept quiet. Whatever was bothering him had to be serious, because she had a distinct feeling he was trying to jog her memory in a roundabout way.

But what was he getting at? What had happened to leave him so resentful? And why blame it all on her? It took two to make an argument.

And two to make a marriage work, she added, hoping he would continue to drop clues to their past difficulties till she'd figured out what he was trying to tell her. Why he didn't just blurt it out she had no idea. If he was as angry as he let on, then why continue to attempt to shield her from pain?

That thought lifted Sandy's spirits. If there was nothing left between them, then why should Wade care if he tormented her? Why not simply fill in the missing details and be done with it, no matter who got hurt?

Because he loves me! she reasoned, the conclusion giving her goose bumps on her arms and raising the hair on the back of her neck. Casting a surreptitious glance his way, she noted the hard line to his jaw, the way his muscles flexed when he drove, his careful concentration on the road ahead rather than taking any notice of her.

Intent on getting his full attention, she said, "Wade...?"

"What?" Still he didn't turn.

"Do you love me?" To Sandy's relief, that question did change his focus.

Wide-eyed, he cast her a withering glance. "Do I *what?*"

"Love me. You know, like before."

"No way."

"I don't believe you," she countered. "If you didn't care, you'd tell me all about our divorce even if it hurt me to have to listen."

"Hmm. You may have a point." Thoughtful, he hesitated before commenting more on her candid observation. "I guess the reason is, since you got hit in the head, you've been a different person. But do I love you the way I did before? The answer is definitely no."

"So, you do love me?"

"I didn't say that, either. What I meant was, you and I can never go back to where we were and recapture the special feelings we used to share."

"Why not?"

Wade's jaw clenched, the muscles in his cheek working. "Because it's impossible—that's all."

"But..."

"*No*, Sandra," he said loudly, firmly. "You and I had our chance and we blew it. End of story."

"Maybe it's time to rewrite the ending," she offered, keeping her voice calm and forcing her tense body to relax as much as possible so she could present a nonthreatening posture. The instant Wade looked over at her and she read the rebuttal in his eyes, she was sorry she had pressed him so hard.

"Give it up," he said. "You can't fix anything if there's nothing left to work with."

"I don't believe that."

Wade's hands tightened on the steering wheel, his knuckles whitening from the pressure. "You don't have to," he said, his tone resolute. "It's enough that I do."

Determined to at least pretend they were happy together, Sandy busied herself in the kitchen as soon as they got home, even cleaning up the pots and pans she'd left from earlier culinary endeavors. If that didn't impress her grumpy ex-husband, she figured nothing would.

Wade had gone outside, ostensibly to mow the back lawn, although Sandy suspected his absence was more a matter of self-preservation than it was an urge to beautify the landscaping.

Scrubbing the last pot, she gazed out the window over the sink, admiring the solitude and attractiveness of the shady, fenced yard. Hummingbird feeders hung from the branches of a fruitless mulberry tree and wisteria grew in a gnarled vine up the side of the patio cover and onto the garage roof.

The scene was so totally familiar and heartwarming it brought tears to her eyes.

We'll put a swing under the tree for the kids, she recalled Wade saying sometime in the distant past. Sandy closed her eyes and let the sweet memory flow through her.

They'd been sitting on the thick, green grass in the shade of the largest tree, admiring the sunset and dreaming of their rosy future. Wade's head was resting in her lap and she was stroking his hair.

"I want at least four children," she remembered responding.

"Not all at once!"

They had both laughed then, following the moment of frivolous joy with a light, romantic kiss. "I love you, Mr. Walker," she said.

Wade reached up and pulled her closer. "I love you, too, Mrs. Walker. Now that we're officially married, don't you think it would be nice to make love right here and now, like this?" His hand was inching up under the full skirt of her sundress.

"Have I ever turned you down?" Sandy teased.

"Many times!"

"I mean since the wedding."

"Well . . ."

She lay down next to him and pillowed her head on his shoulder. "What's wrong with going into the house and finding a nice, soft bed?"

"Where's your spirit of adventure?" Wade asked, kissing her till she had no breath left for an answer.

Sandy held him tightly, ignoring everything but the hard press of his masculine body and the tantalizing idea of actually making love out under the stars in the privacy of the enclosed backyard. One of the things she liked most about her husband was his élan, his zest for living life to the utmost and taking advantage of unique opportunities for happiness, no matter where or when they occurred.

Wade's practiced hands traveled up her back, then down again, to push away the folds of her skirt and settle on her hips. He pulled her to him with a vigor enhanced by lusty need and the added excitement of actually making her his right there under the tree.

Rolling over so Sandy was on the bottom, he braced himself above her. "I can't help myself. I need you, honey."

"I need you, too, Wade." She reached for him, looped her arms around his neck and pulled him down on top of her for another long, erotic kiss. By the time they broke for air, Sandy was so overcome with the wonder of their mutual hunger she was barely able to speak.

Keeping their lips joined, he was writhing against her, pushing aside the clothing that was the only remaining barrier to their oneness. She felt his manhood, hot and hard, press against her for an instant, before they were joined with a quick, sure thrust.

All that mattered at that precious moment was the two of them and their marvelous love. Sandy rejoiced in the knowledge that she finally belonged, finally had someone whom she could trust implicitly and rely upon in any circumstance, no matter how dire.

Celebrating that awareness and the inner peace it brought, she had lifted her legs and wrapped them around him, matching every surge with one of her own till they were soaring with the stars, then shooting back to earth in a shower of brightly colored meteors to lie panting on the grass and clinging to each other, unwilling to let go. It was a moment of timeless rapture, the perfect example of two people madly, ecstatically, in love.

Palms sweaty, mouth dry, Sandy leaned heavily against the sink and shuddered at the vividness of the memory. That night should have been one of the most exquisite times of her life, but it *wasn't*, she realized with a start. In fact, the moment the intense images of their union began to fade from her mind, they were replaced with a sadness so deep it left a tangible ache in her core.

Do I want to remember all of it? she wondered, turning away from the window and staring blankly. *If it already hurts this much, do I really want to know the rest?*

Chapter Thirteen

After the upsetting recollection about making love beneath the mulberry tree, Sandy was left with a yearning to be back in Wade's arms that refused to go away no matter how hard she tried to distract herself. Finally she decided to change into something sexy in the hope that he would at least kiss her again.

Although she hadn't consciously planned on a seduction attempt, she had brought along a gauzy blouse and matching skirt that he had given her shortly after their marriage. The outfit was pale pink with a scooped neckline gathered by a thin, satin ribbon. Untying the bow and leaving the ends of the ribbon hanging loose bared the top swell of her breasts and left little to the imagination. Naturally that was how she wore it.

When Wade came back inside from his stint with the lawn mower, she was waiting with a glass of cold iced tea and a smile. To her consternation, he accepted the drink and ignored what she was wearing in spite of the low-cut neckline and feminine, flowing skirt.

"I've got to have a shower," he said flatly, wiping perspiration off his forehead, then taking a big draft of the icy liquid. "Had any luck finding Jane Ellen yet?"

Sandy wasn't about to admit she'd spent her time daydreaming and changing clothes to impress him. "No. Not yet."

"Why don't you go use the phone in the den? It's private and that way we won't bother each other."

What could she say? *I'd rather stay where you can see me so you'll take the hint and ravage me the way you used to?* Hardly. She scanned his body with undisguised desire. The heat and sunshine had given his muscles a tanned sheen that highlighted them beautifully, making them look the way bodybuilders' muscles did in competition. Slim-waisted, he moved with the grace of an athlete, even though he was obviously tired. Sandy sighed. What a shame he was being such a prude.

A blush rose to embrace her cheeks and she looked away so Wade could not read the primitive need in her eyes. What had come over her? She used to be the one who insisted they not have sex outside of marriage, and here she was, lusting after the man as if she were the most wanton woman on earth. Why?

Because I still feel married to him, she answered. Of course. That was it. He might remember their splitting up and subsequent divorce, but she had absolutely no inkling of what had happened. Consequently it was perfectly normal for her to think of him as accessible. It might not be morally correct at present, but wanting her husband to make love to her was definitely still an important aspect of her psyche, one she was unable to deny.

The question was, did she dare act on her most basic urges if Wade did eventually succumb to her charms?

Looking up, she saw that he had gone, leaving her alone with her lurid thoughts. "Apparently I won't have to decide anytime soon," she muttered with a scowl. Making her

way to the den, she began to dial the numbers in her address book.

Sandy had worked her way from *A* to *W* by dinnertime
that evening. Either half the phones had answering ma-
chines hooked up to them or the information in the book
was outdated and useless.

Discouraged, she joined Wade on the couch in the den for
a dinner of take-out Chinese he'd had delivered to the
house. He'd opened the white, paper containers and set
them, along with plates, forks and napkins, on the coffee
table before he summoned her.

"No luck?" he asked, handing her a plate and napkin.

Sandy shook her head as she took a seat beside him and
smoothed her skirt on her lap. "Not much. Apparently I'm
not as organized as I thought. A lot of the information in
the address book is obsolete."

"Yeah, well..." Wade shrugged. "You can try again after dinner. More people should be home then."

"I guess so." Scooping fried rice onto her plate, she followed it with a generous helping of Mongolian beef and
cashew chicken, then passed the containers to him. "You
could save me all this hassle, you know. All you have to do
is tell me about our divorce and be done with it."

Looking at her soberly, he tried to smile. "Sure. And
you'd think I was making it all up."

"I would not."

"Oh? You didn't believe anybody about your job or
apartment."

"That was different."

"Really? How?"

"Well..." Sandy took a bite of her beef and paused to
chew. "I was more confused back then. I really do think I'm
better now." She noticed Wade was giving her a funny look,
his gaze centering on her lips. "What's wrong?"

He reached out and gently brushed a tiny, white noodle fragment off the corner of her mouth, his thumb lingering far longer than necessary. The simple gesture became a caress.

Sandy held perfectly still, her eyes wide, her pulse beating wildly. His thumb was slightly calloused from hard work, yet his touch was so tender it was barely a whisper on her soft skin.

"I got it," he finally said, his voice hoarse and rasping. "We need something to drink with all this. What would you like?"

"Water is fine, thanks." She couldn't believe how rapidly and skillfully he managed to subvert the fondness that was so evident in his touch, in his eyes. Every cell in her body was screaming for fulfillment and all Wade wanted to know was what beverage she'd like with her meal. The man had to be made of concrete and iron instead of flesh and bone! Where were his feelings? His true emotions? Was it too late to reach him the way she used to? She hoped not.

Sandy smiled as he returned with two glasses of ice water. "Thanks."

"You're welcome." He eyed her plate. "You're not eating. Don't you like it?"

"It's fine. Actually it tastes very familiar. I suppose this kind of ethnic food is one of my favorites and I'm too dense to remember loving it."

"Something like that."

"Too bad I didn't also forget loving you," she said, fully intending to make him aware that her emotions might be jumbled but some of them were nevertheless quite clear.

Wade jammed a forkful of food into his mouth, chewed with a vengeance, then said, "Don't start."

"Why not?" Ignoring what little was left of her appetite, Sandy sat back from her plate and looked over at him, her fingers toying nervously with the ends of the satin ribbons on her blouse. "For your sake, I've spent the past few

days trying to disregard the way I feel, and where has it
gotten me?" She glanced down at the softly feminine outfit
Wade had continued to ignore. "You're acting as if I were
Attila the Hun in drag."

The outrageous suggestion brought a smile to Wade's lips
in spite of his determination to remain indifferent. "I think
he was a lot taller. Besides, you don't have a beard."

"Details, details," Sandy quipped. "My point is, I seem
to be in love with you, at least from a sentimental perspec-
tive, and I figured it wouldn't hurt to say so."

"What good does it do?" Wade countered. "You're just
going to make yourself miserable and embarrassed in the
long run."

"I've been that way before and it hasn't killed me." Gazing unseeing across the room, she thought back to her earlier reverie in the kitchen and asked, "Do you remember
making love to me outside under the mulberry tree, or did I
conjure up that scene in my imagination?"

Wade immediately stiffened and inched away from her.
"Why? What do you think you remember?"

"Not much." Sandy felt a warm blush flowing up her
cheeks. "Well, enough. It's just that I can't shake off a
mood of sadness about it and that kind of reaction doesn't
seem to make any sense."

"It will."

"I'm not going to like what I find out, am I?"

"You didn't seem too upset at the time."

There was no doubt in her mind that Wade was fighting
to maintain his self-control. Whatever had taken place under the tree obviously had a direct bearing on their marital
woes, yet no amount of thinking, wishing or praying
brought more details back to her.

But I was close to knowing, she told herself. *And the rest
of the story will come to me. I know it will.*

She gazed over at Wade. His posture was rigid, his expression drawn and tense. The way he was staring at her, his

darkly mysterious gaze holding both indictment and re-
sentment, she felt as if she were on trial. Too bad she was the
only person in the pseudo-courtroom who had no idea what
she was being accused of or how to defend herself.

Under so much seemingly undeserved pressure, Sandy
decided to leave the room and go somewhere private to
think. Not that it would do her any good, she reasoned
wryly, but who cared? All she knew was, she had to distance herself from the bleak, distressing mood that was
permeating the otherwise cheery room.

It wasn't enough simply to go into the kitchen or bedroom for solace, either. The whole house was closing in on
her and making her feel as if she had to get away, no matter
what. Suddenly escape was the only perception, the only
focus, in her mind. Wide-eyed, she jumped to her feet and
stared at Wade.

"Sit down and finish your dinner," he ordered.

"I'm not hungry."

"You still have to eat. Look, Sandy, I'm sorry I snapped
at you, okay? You just have to try to see things my way.
Having you here isn't easy."

"You think it is for me?"

"I don't know. Is it?"

"No!"

Wade eyed her trembling figure beneath the gauzy outfit. "No? Then why dress like that? Are you trying to drive
me crazy or are you on some kind of self-destructive mis-
sion?"

"I didn't think you noticed," she said, wondering how
long he'd been hiding his reactions and marveling at how
well he did it. "You're a real expert at acting like you don't
care, aren't you?"

"That's because I don't," Wade lied, hoping she'd accept the fabrication.

"Fine. Then you won't mind if I get some air."

Her sandals made little sound as she stomped to the foyer, yanked open the front door and darted out onto the porch and down the steps, hoping against hope that Wade would not follow her this time.

Invisible forces pressed down on her, making it hard to breathe, hard to think. In the far recesses of her troubled mind, she recognized guilt about some undefined sin, then realized there was also adamant denial attached to it.

Sandy leaned heavily against the metal post that held the colonial-style light illuminating the front walk. "I didn't do anything wrong," she whispered to the silent stars. "I know I didn't."

Closing her eyes to blot out everything but her stormy emotions, she fought back tears of frustration and prayed she was right.

The moon rose like an icy blue crescent in a misty sea of unshed tears. Thankful that Wade had remained inside the house and was showing no sign of bothering her, Sandy slowly began to relax.

She could always drive the station wagon back to her apartment, she thought, immediately discounting the idea. It was awful to be alone while still disoriented. Even angry, Wade provided a haven against all the unseen demons from her past. He always had.

Thinking back, Sandy pictured the peaceful garden scene she had merely glimpsed days before. This time the vision came more easily, its details intense, its joyous mood unmistakable.

Wade was wearing a pearl-gray tuxedo and waiting for her at the end of a long, white runner that had been placed on the grass in the lovely outdoor setting. Although not exactly the same, the garden was vaguely reminiscent of the backyard of the house where he now lived.

Violet was present, of course, as was Sandy's father, although his image was distant and faded. Wearing a lavender-colored, designer ensemble, the older woman was fussing over the way the sheer, white veil draped over the satin-and-lace shoulders of Sandy's wedding gown.

"It's fine, Mother. Leave it alone."

"It is not." She made a sour face. "I don't know why you couldn't have waited at least until after graduation to do this. You aren't pregnant, are you?"

Sandy laughed. "Not unless you believe in miracles. I told you, Wade and I have *not* slept together."

"Then what's the hurry? I could have given you a marvelous gala if I'd had more time to prepare."

"We didn't want a big party, Mother. I told you that." She glanced over at the dim visage of her father. "I'm just glad Daddy could make it."

"It's a wonder, considering the rush. You don't think of anyone but yourself, Sandra. You never have. I don't know where I went wrong in raising you."

You might have tried staying sober, Sandy thought, refusing to give vent to her feelings and spoil the day more than it already was.

Unfortunately, Violet was far from finished with her tirade. She pointed a thin, manicured finger up the aisle to where Wade waited. "That man is going to be the ruin of you, Sandra. You'll see. First thing you know you'll be pregnant and there goes your degree. I simply can't believe you're doing this after all the hard work you put in to get through college."

"We're not having children right away," Sandy reassured her. "Wade has agreed to let me finish school first, even if I decide to go on for my master's. He's very supportive."

"Hah! So was your father till he got me into bed. Men are like that, I tell you. They can't be trusted." She sniffled and patted her nose with a lace-edged hankie. "I could have been a success on my own, you know, if I hadn't gotten married and had you so quickly."

"Yes, Mother, I know," Sandy said with as much compassion as she could muster. The story was an old, often-repeated one. The words changed from time to time, but the theme remained constant: children were unwanted and wrecked your life, as did marriage. What a sad outlook.

Sighing, Sandy watched her mother be seated, then joined her father and started down the white runner toward Wade and the future she knew would contain all the happiness she had been denied as a little girl. Tears filled her eyes. The sight of him was so precious, so like a beautiful dream.

She smiled, her joy meant only for him. His thick hair was combed neatly back, his cheeks shaved clean of the shadowy stubble that she thought made him appear so roguish and exciting.

Returning her grin, he looked proud to be taking her as his bride, that realization making her heart stop for a thrilling instant. This was her moment. Her man. A familiar heat curled inside her. Strong and sure of himself, he stood waiting. For her. For the future they had planned so carefully. She had never felt so wanted, so validated, in her entire life.

The music peaked, then died down. Pausing beside Wade, Sandy reached out and took his hand, leaving the father she had never really belonged to and joining with the one man who gave her life meaning. This was mortal existence at its zenith, she mused. This was reaching for perfection and finding it.

Gazing up at him and smiling, she felt a surge of panic. Her heart began to race. Wade's image was fading. In its place stood a cold stone statue made in his likeness.

Sandy blinked. The beautiful euphoria surrounding her began to wane, pulling back a little at a time like the relentless ebbing of the tide. Left in her conscious mind was the sure knowledge that they had been happy for a short while. Deliriously happy. And then . . .

Tears slid silently down her cheeks. Then it had ended in divorce. But why? Why?

Clouds covered one corner of the crescent moon, making the night seem less welcoming. Spent from weeping, her emotions once again under control, Sandy decided to go back into the house and try to enjoy what was left of the evening. At the rate she was regaining lost memories, her time with Wade was surely limited and she wanted to make the most of what remained.

I won't ask any more questions, she told herself. *We get along better when I don't, and the truth will come to me soon enough.*

Turning, she made her way back to the porch steps, hesitating when the haunting fragrance of tea roses reached her, the unexpected sweetness making her feel good all over.

In the stillness, the scent of the tiny, pink blossoms wafted through the air, beckoning her to come closer. As if greeting an old friend, Sandy approached and reached out her hand to carefully caress the soft petals of the nearest rose.

It was petite and delicate, as were all the flowers on that particular bush. Blooming profusely, the bush was climbing up the side of the house on a trellis, its long shoots winding around the wooden framework and spilling out in a cascade of beauty and fragrance.

Enchanted by the roses, Sandy plucked a few of the largest blossoms and made them into a bouquet in her hand, wondering if the melancholy she was beginning to feel had anything to do with having had the same kind of flowers in her bridal bouquet.

Or maybe Wade had given her pink roses and that was why these touched her heart so poignantly, she mused. Smiling slightly at the pleasant thought, she added a few sprigs of greenery from a nearby diosma bush and started for the house once more, her treasures in hand, her spirit calmed.

What should she say to Wade to break the ice? Sandy wondered. Perhaps it would be best just to go quietly up to

him and present him with the bouquet she'd made and hope
it was an adequate peace offering.

The unusual idea struck her as splendid. Even though
men were not supposed to appreciate flowers the way
women did, she somehow knew he loved that particular
rosebush and would be pleased to see its lovely, fragrant
blooms. Entering the house, she followed the sound of
clattering pans and running water coming from the kitchen.

Wade had put away the dinner leftovers and was busy
straightening up. Hiding the bouquet behind her, she walked
slowly into the room and smiled at him. "Hi."

He jumped as if he'd been shocked by electricity. "Oh.
You're back."

"Yes. Thanks for letting me have my privacy. I had some
serious thinking to do and I needed to be alone."

"That's what I figured. I watched out the window for a
few minutes and you seemed to be doing okay." He waited,
studying her face. "You look as if you've worked out some
of your problems."

"I have." Sandy's smile grew. "I've decided to stop pes-
tering you for answers and just let nature take its course.
The way I'm improving, it shouldn't be long before I remember everything."

A deep sigh raised Wade's shoulders, then dropped them
with a shudder. "Good. I may live after all."

"Having me around can't be *that* bad," Sandy quipped.

"*Difficult* is a better choice of words."

Stepping closer, she nodded with understanding. "You've
been great through all this, Wade. Whatever happens, I
want you to know that."

"Thanks." Her soft-voiced sincerity tore at his facade of
indifference, making him struggle to keep from reaching out
and pulling her into his arms for one last, farewell embrace. Soon she would be going, and he sensed his body's
unwillingness to let her walk away.

"I brought you something," Sandy said, revealing the bouquet. "I was outside and I remembered how you loved these roses, so I picked some for the house."

Wade stiffened, his hands closing into fists as he stared, unbelieving, at the tiny flowers. Harsh condemnation took the place of the tenderness he had been experiencing and he snapped at her. "How dare you?"

"How dare I what? Pick your flowers?" She was instantly filled with anxiety and dismay. "Don't be silly. There are hundreds of these on the climbing bush outside. What difference can a few less make?"

"Don't tell me you don't know, Sandra. If you've come this far, then you're cured. What you just did was cruel and unfeeling, even for you." Snatching the frail bouquet from her hand, he hurled it to the floor. "Get out of my sight."

Taken aback, Sandy began to edge away from him and make her way toward the door. "What did I do?"

"Get out of here!"

"Why? Tell me why!"

Shaking with repressed emotion, Wade repeated his demands. "Go away. Leave me."

Sandy didn't fear him, even though he was shouting at her. Listening to the catch in his voice and seeing the unshed tears filling his eyes, she knew for certain Wade was distraught, which made him pitiable rather than dangerous.

She eyed the poor, discarded roses lying scattered on the floor. They seemed so pathetic, like little children stripped of a loving family and callously cast away to be forgotten.

Her heart leaped to her throat. Why had she suddenly thought of the pink roses as synonymous with lost children? Surely she had never been a mother or lost a baby, had she? Or *had* she?

Dashing from the room, she grabbed her purse off the hall table and fumbled in it for her car keys as she ran out into the night. The idea that she and Wade might have once conceived a child should be totally foreign to her, yet it wasn't, and that unmistakable clue to the past left her trembling and shaken.

The roses are a symbol, she suddenly realized. *Wade and I planted that bush together when we were struggling to accept a terrible loss! And now he thinks I was taunting him with the bouquet. Oh, dear God!*

Sandy started her car and jammed it into reverse gear. Temporarily spotlit by the beam of her headlights, the tiny pink roses seemed to glow for an instant, then disappear.

Like the fleeting life of the baby who was never born, she thought. Tears filled her eyes and slid down her cheeks as the memory washed over her and tore at her broken heart.

"It wasn't my fault," she shouted into the stillness. "It couldn't have been. I'd never do anything to harm a helpless little baby!"

The secret guilt she had been harboring broke free and tried to overwhelm her, but failed. The miscarriage hadn't been due to any shortcomings or omissions on her part. She knew that as surely as she knew she had once been pregnant with her husband's baby.

Wade was the one who could never accept the loss as being a natural occurrence, she recalled, seeing his pain all over again and sensing her inability to relieve it no matter how hard she'd tried.

He'd blamed her for continuing with school while pregnant and then losing the baby. When she'd tried to explain, he had refused to listen, even when her obstetrician had gone into medical detail that totally exonerated her.

And then Wade had filed for divorce, Sandy recollected with a sharp surge of true anguish and a flood of tears. She was innocent, yet he had blamed her for everything, simply because he didn't trust her enough to accept that she had done nothing wrong.

It was the lack of trust that had hurt the worst. She would have given her life to make him believe in her again.

Sobbing inconsolably, she pulled the station wagon to the curb, put her head on the wheel and wept.

Chapter Fourteen

Wade bent to pick up the dying roses. They lay in his palm, their weight so slight he could hardly feel anything. Which was a pretty good description of the numb condition of his heart, too, he thought wryly.

It had been Sandy's idea to plant the rosebush in remembrance of their child. He'd gone along with the plan only because that was what his wife wanted. At that time, he'd been prone to take the line of least resistance about nearly everything, so when she'd come home with the plant one day he'd simply dug the hole for her and stood back to watch with little feeling and no enthusiasm.

Sandy was on her knees in the dirt, holding the rosebush gingerly by its base. "Don't you want to help?"

Wade remembered shaking his head. "No. You do it."

"Please?"

There was no doubt the symbolic act was affecting her emotionally and Wade wasn't sure he wanted to take part when she'd been the cause of the grief in the first place. "I said no."

"Oh, Wade. Don't be that way."

"What way?"

"You know, mad at me. The doctor explained it all. I would have lost our baby even if I'd stayed in bed all the time. My hormones were all messed up from when I tried to take those birth-control pills."

"Right. Too bad you quit."

He recalled her tenseness then, and the anguish reflected in her eyes as she said, "You know they made me sick. That was why we agreed to use other methods instead of trying to find a prescription I could take without having bad side effects."

"Yeah." Wade grabbed the shovel handle and bent to scoop up some dirt. "Just put that thing where you want it and let's get this over with, okay? Art called while you were gone. I've got to get back to work."

Placing the bush gently into the ground, Sandy had watered it with her tears as he refilled the hole. Wade recalled that he, too, had wept, although not then, not where she could see his weakness.

As time passed, the delicate-looking plant grew robust and began to bloom profusely. Now, every time he saw it, Wade wondered what his son might have been like had he been given the same chance at life, the same tender, loving care.

"It really *wasn't* her fault," he murmured, remembering the soul-deep pain in Sandy's eyes when he'd shouted at her and ordered her out of his house. Frankly, he was the one who had gotten her pregnant under false pretenses and therefore the blame for the tragedy had to be shouldered equally.

In time, Wade knew he probably would have accepted that plain truth, but by the time his heart had begun to soften, it was too late. Their divorce was final and she was gone.

His fist closed around the tiny, pink blossoms, breaking the frail petals from the stems and letting them fall silently to the floor at his feet while he cursed himself and lamented the grudge he'd been harboring for way too long.

Hurting Sandy once for her supposed transgressions wasn't enough, was it? Oh, no. He'd gone and done it again, simply because he'd never made a real effort to forgive and to readjust his instinctive responses to her.

She'd said she loved him, and in return he'd treated her abominably! Wade tilted his head back and closed his eyes. What an idiot he'd been. Having her there, in his house, had been the gift of a second chance, and he'd blown it as surely as if it had never happened.

Moisture filled his eyes and he blinked it back, willing himself to calm down and try to think with his head instead of his heart. Maybe it wasn't too late. Maybe there was one more miracle due him, although why, he couldn't imagine. He didn't deserve another chance any more than he deserved to have the love of a special woman like Sandy. Especially not after all he'd said and done to hurt her.

"Oh, hell," Wade mumbled, heading for the door with the intention of following her and begging for the chance to try again. "What do I have to lose? All she can do is tell me she never wants to see me again."

That awful thought made him shiver all the way to his core.

Sandy drove mindlessly through the streets of Riverside. Everything was beginning to look familiar, even the buildings she knew had been built since she and Wade had lived there. Yes, this was home, she admitted with reluctance. The roads leading to her apartment were a recognizable part of her regular, daily routine.

Thank goodness she'd had vacation time lined up before she'd gotten hurt, she thought, wondering exactly when she was due back at work and not really caring. Nothing mat-

tered much. Not now. Wade had been right when he'd told
her it would be hard to adjust to the present after being so
convinced she was living in the past. Sandy sighed. Boy,
when he was right, he was dead right.

The last thing she wanted to do was drive home to face an
empty apartment, yet she had nowhere else to go except for
her parents' house, and she decided she'd rather sleep in the
car than show up there and listen to another of her mother's lectures.

Turning left on Chicago Avenue, she headed back toward Glenwood, her head spinning with the events of the
past few days. Thankfully, throughout the ordeal, she had
at least known who she was. More important, it was a
darned good thing she now knew who she was *not*. Trying
to seduce a man who was no longer your husband could lead
to all sorts of complications. The last thing she needed at
this point in her life was another impossible predicament
with no way out.

Like loving Wade, she admitted, heaving a deep, telling
sigh. Had she not admitted her infatuation to him in such a
graphic manner, it would be a lot easier to walk away.

But I'd still be in love with him. Sandy nodded sadly. *Yes.*
In spite of everything that had happened, both in the past
and recently, she loved Wade Walker with all her heart. All
she could hope was that eventually that love would fade
enough to let her find someone else.

In the back of her mind, where the secrets of her soul lay
shrouded, she seriously doubted it.

Wade drove directly to Sandy's apartment. Taking the
stairs two at a time, he reached the second-floor landing and
began pounding on her door.

"Sandy," he called as loudly as he felt he dared due to the
late hour. "It's me. I'm sorry for everything. Please, let me
in."

When there was no response, he tried twice more, then went to the only window facing the hallway and knocked on the glass. "Sandra, please. I know you're in there."

But was she? Peering through the sheer curtains in the center of the windowpanes, he cupped his hand around his eyes so he could see better. The place looked exactly as it had when they were there together, which told him nothing, he realized with chagrin.

His mind was spinning. The station wagon! Of course. He'd been in such a hurry to get to her, he hadn't checked the parking structure to see if her car was there. What if she hadn't come home? Worse yet, what if she'd had a relapse and something bad had happened to her?

Growing more frantic with every negative thought, Wade ran down the stairs to the numbered stalls. One quick look told him the parking place designated for Sandy's apartment was empty.

Fiercely distraught and totally at a loss as to how to proceed, he could barely keep from cupping his hands around his mouth and shouting her name to the heavens as he ran back to his truck and sped off to search for her.

Chapter Fifteen

Weary beyond sensibility, and tired of hours of mindless driving, Sandy climbed the stairs to her apartment and unlocked the door. All her personal belongings and furniture were exactly as they should be, she noted, including the striped wallpaper and the bedroom suite that had been so unfamiliar such a short while before.

She dropped her purse on a chair. The suitcase full of clothes was still at Wade's and could stay there as far as she was concerned. So could he. It was hard enough just to think about him. Actually putting herself in the same room or the same house with that man again was out of the question.

Which probably went double for him, she added, her conscience reminding her that he had indeed taken her in and looked after her when she could think of no one else to ask for help.

Sandy's stomach churned, her body rebelling against the traumatic events of the past hours. Poor Wade. He must have gone through pure hell when she was kissing him and asking him to make love to her. Not that he didn't enjoy himself, she countered, hoping that idea would salve her conscience.

It didn't. Disgusted with herself for being careless and having the accident that had caused her to lose her memory in the first place, Sandy gingerly felt for the lump on her scalp. Except for a tiny scratch where her head had hit the edge of the ditch, she found nothing. Which was just as well, since her medicine was also at Wade's.

Pensive, Sandy sat down on the sofa, slipped off her sandals and propped her feet on the coffee table, closing her eyes and laying back her head to free the last of her hidden memories.

It had been spring then, too. Nearly time for her college graduation. She hadn't been feeling well for several weeks and had gone to the doctor for a checkup, hoping to find out what was wrong and renew her strength in time for final exams.

Sandy's hand drifted to her abdomen, and she fantasized about the miniature person who had once resided there for such a short time. To begin with, she hadn't known how she felt about having a baby, but a few days after hearing the doctor's diagnosis, the idea had taken root and she was nearly as cheerful about the prospect of parenthood as Wade.

"I thought men weren't supposed to be happy about being tied down," she remembered saying.

"I guess I'm not typical."

His grin was so wide and comical she couldn't help giggling. "That has been mentioned."

"By your mother, no doubt," he said. "Have you broken the good news to her yet?"

"No." Sandy sobered. "I know what she's going to say and I have no desire to listen to her tirade. I've heard it so often I can recite it by heart."

Wade folded her gently in his arms. "She's wrong, you know. Children aren't the end of life—they're the beginning. You'll see. I'll show you what it's like to belong to a real family, honey."

"I know. I just wish I'd finished school before this happened."

"You still can. Even if you want to go on and sign up for more classes later. I'll make arrangements to take the little one to work with me and you can have the whole day free to study or whatever."

"Except for the next seven or eight months," she corrected. "Those are all mine."

"When it starts to show, I swear I'll love you no matter how chubby you get," Wade told her, caressing her flat abdomen.

"Promises, promises. Jane Ellen swears there's a lot more to being pregnant than just getting big around the middle. Going into hard labor is a particularly interesting concept."

"I'll rub your back when it hurts and let you call me all sorts of ugly names while you're having the baby," he vowed.

Sandy chuckled. "You've been talking to Jane's husband about this, haven't you?"

"Guilty. And if I'm not worried, you certainly shouldn't be. I'm with you all the way, honey."

Sandy paused, her brow furrowing. "You know, one thing puzzles me."

"What's that?"

"How this happened."

"Well," Wade said, his voice a slow, sexy drawl, "first you and I went to bed together and then..."

"Not *that* part."

"Oh. Then what's the question?"

"We always used some form of birth control, even on our honeymoon, so how did I get pregnant?"

He acted uncomfortable with the question, pausing, stepping away from her and thrusting his hands into his pockets before he answered. "Um, I'm not sure, but remember the time we made love outside under the mulberry tree?"

Sighing, Sandy hugged herself. "Do I! That was some romantic idea you had."

"I agree. The trouble is, I didn't have any protection with me and I sort of . . . well . . ."

"You *faked* it?" She vividly recalled his momentary pause before he entered her and her gullible assumption that he was duly taking care of the necessary precautions. "Damn it, I trusted you! How could you do this to me, especially right now? You know how much my degree means!"

"Of course I do. I didn't get you pregnant on purpose. The odds were against it. I gambled and lost. It's not the end of the world, for crying out loud."

"Not for you maybe," she shouted back.

"It isn't for you, either," Wade countered. "You're not your mother—you're my wife. There's no comparison."

"Except that she got pregnant with me while she was in school and has blamed me for her shortcomings ever since."

Calming himself, he reached out to touch her arm and brought her back into the comforting embrace they both needed. "Well, she's wrong. You and I both know that. Children are a gift from God, not a penance from the devil. Our child will be loved, and know it every day of his life."

Sandy remembered the affectionate way he'd stroked her cheek then, caressing it with his warm palm. "And if it's a girl?"

"She'll be spoiled rotten, just like her mama, when I get through with the pair of you. I love you, Sandy. With all my heart and soul. I always will."

Bringing her thoughts back to the present, she tried to stop herself from reliving another part of their past—three days she wished she could wipe from her mind. That was when the physical pain had started for no apparent reason, to be followed by an emotional anguish far greater than any she could have imagined.

In spite of all Wade's wonderful promises and early show of support he had unjustly blamed her for the spontaneous loss of his baby, apparently convinced she'd consciously wanted to rid herself of the inconvenience because of her single-minded devotion to getting her degree.

"You didn't want to be pregnant," he'd shouted. "Admit it."

"No! Yes. Oh, I don't know," Sandy had wailed. "It doesn't matter. It's over with and neither of us can change what happened."

It was then that she'd raced off in the yellow Mustang and wrecked it against a light pole when tears had blurred her vision so much that she'd missed a curve in the road. Thank goodness no one was hurt in the accident.

Bending under the crush of memories so vivid they made her hurt all over, she spoke as if her husband were present to hear her wholehearted lament.

"I did all I could to keep the baby," Sandy whispered. "I needed you so much then, Wade. The doctor told you over and over again that it wasn't my fault. Why couldn't you believe in me? Why?"

Ignoring the sparse tears that trickled down her cheeks, Sandy turned off the lamp beside the couch, closed her eyes and eventually drifted off into dreamless sleep.

*   *   *

Wade had driven everywhere he could imagine Sandy might have gone, including Rossmore Elementary. Periodic sweeps past her apartment building to look for her car had netted him nothing until 3:00 a.m. when he noticed the station wagon had returned.

Oh, God, let her be okay, he prayed, skidding to a stop and jumping from his truck. He was up the stairs and bursting through her door in mere seconds.

In the darkened room, he saw a shadow seated on the couch, unmoving.

"Sandy!" Wade shouted, hurling himself at her without any thought for propriety. All he could think of was touching her and holding her in his arms to reassure himself she was all right.

Sandy, however, awakened to glimpse a huge, dark shape descending on her from the open doorway. The instant she drew a breath, she let out a scream that rattled the windows and gave Wade the shakes even though he knew there was nothing wrong.

"It's okay," he said as he fell to his knees in front of her and reached out. "It's me."

Surrounded by the bedlam from the crashing door, her own frantic screams and the thunderous pounding of her heart, Sandy was slow to recognize the deep voice. Striking out with all her strength and kicking furiously, she connected with her attacker's nose, ribs and one ear, hearing him grunt with surprise and pain.

He grasped her wrists and pinned her to the sofa, holding fast while she struggled to free herself. "Sandy, no!" he shouted. "It's me. Wade."

The words filtered through the haze of remaining sleep to touch her heart and make her gasp. "Wade?"

"Yes." Releasing her cautiously, he gingerly explored his face as she flicked on the light. There were drops of blood on his hand when he looked down at it. "I think you broke my nose."

"Your nose? *Your nose?* You scared me to *death!*"

"Not as much as you scared me when you disappeared tonight."

"You were worried about me?" The concept gave her an undeniable thrill.

"Of course I was. What if something had happened to you?" He dabbed at his sore nose. "Jeez, what a wallop."

Sandy pressed her fingertips to her lips to stifle a giggle brought on by intense relief from her initial fear and the added joy of awaking to see him kneeling subjectively at her feet.

"I'll...I'll get you a towel," she said, starting for the kitchen. "Wait here."

"Not on your life."

She sensed that Wade was right behind her and she could hardly make herself continue walking away. Whatever had brought him there had also compelled him to practically break down her door and then fling himself bodily at her. If that didn't mean he cared a lot more than he'd admitted before, she'd turn in her amateur psychologist's certificate.

Wetting a small hand towel, Sandy turned and gently began wiping away the drops of blood on his upper lip. "I don't think there's any serious damage," she said, gazing into his eyes and seeing only love where there had been so much anger and distrust before.

"The damage is what I did to you two years ago," Wade whispered. He closed his hands over hers, stilling them and dropping the damp towel to the floor, unheeded. "I was too stubborn and hurt to think straight, honey, and I wasn't much better when you showed up the other day. I guess I was just in too much of a hurry to prove to you that we could be a real family. I know it wasn't your fault about the baby."

"No, it wasn't." The tears that filled her eyes were those of relief. "I tried to make you understand, but you were so sure I'd lied. That was what was so painful," she went on. "I thought you believed in me."

"I did. I do," Wade told her, his own eyes growing misty. "Can you ever forgive me?"

"Probably."

"When?" He pulled her into his arms and held her tightly, heart to heart.

Sandy tilted her head back and gazed up at him, her every dream fulfilled, her life once again complete. Now that Wade had finally made a gesture of pardon and healing, she wasn't about to play coy and risk spoiling it. Their love was too precious to chance any delay, no matter how reckless it felt to forgive him outright.

She smiled broadly. "How about right now?"

"Do you mean it?"

"Yes. I wasn't kidding when I said I still loved you. Even if I was slightly out of my head at the time, it still goes."

"Oh, honey..." Lowering his mouth to cover hers, he claimed the passion he knew she was offering and felt his ardor returned tenfold.

Sandy pressed her body to his, her thigh finding its place between his, her abdomen knotting with desire and the anticipation of the pleasure she knew they would soon share.

"We have a lot of catching up to do," Wade said. He swept her up in his arms and started across the living room, the hem of her gauzy, pink skirt flowing out behind them.

"Not till you marry me," she warned, her guileful grin seeming to contradict her words.

"You're kidding, right?"

A blindingly bright glare came from the direction of the still-open front door, two flashlight beams sweeping the room till they settled on Wade and the woman he held in his arms.

"All right, mister, drop her," a husky, masculine voice commanded.

Wade stared, openmouthed.

"I said, put her down."

"Okay, okay." Stationing himself between Sandy and the intruders, he prepared to do battle if necessary, although he had a pretty good idea who their nocturnal visitors were.

The overhead lights were switched on to reveal that the two men were indeed police officers, both looking stern and ready for adversity. "What's going on here? We got a call about a woman screaming."

Sandy peeked out from behind Wade and wiggled her fingers in a shy wave, while blushing profusely. "That would be me."

"What's the trouble, miss?"

"It's *Mrs.*, and this is my husband," Sandy said, feeling like a teenager caught necking after curfew and trying to keep from giggling. "There's no trouble."

"Did you scream?"

"Well . . . maybe a little."

Wade slipped his arm around her and pulled her to his side. "We're newlyweds. You guys know how it is. The little woman gets carried away sometimes."

Reassured, the officers nodded, wished them well and went back out the door, closing it behind them and leaving Sandy and Wade alone.

"Little woman!" She elbowed him in the ribs. "How old-fashioned can you get?"

Wade rubbed his side. "Hey, knock it off, or I'll tell them you socked me in the nose."

"Oh, yeah?"

"Yeah," he echoed. "Now, where were we before our uninvited guests showed up?"

"If you've already forgotten, maybe I'd better reconsider the whole thing."

"Not on your life, lady. A promise is a promise. And this time it's for keeps, right?"

"When we get married this time, we *stay* married," Sandy agreed, her heart singing.

She was not at all surprised to hear her loving husband concur without reservation as he kicked the bedroom door shut behind them, lowered her onto the bed and started to kiss her with more passion and tenderness than ever before.

*   *   *   *   *

The first book in the exciting new
Fortune's Children series is
HIRED HUSBAND
by *New York Times* bestselling writer
Rebecca Brandewyne

Beginning in July 1996
Only from Silhouette Books

Here's an exciting sneak preview....

Minneapolis, Minnesota

As Caroline Fortune wheeled her dark blue Volvo into the underground parking lot of the towering, glass-and-steel structure that housed the global headquarters of Fortune Cosmetics, she glanced anxiously at her gold Piaget wristwatch. An accident on the snowy freeway had caused rush-hour traffic to be a nightmare this morning. As a result, she was running late for her 9:00 a.m. meeting—and if there was one thing her grandmother, Kate Winfield Fortune, simply couldn't abide, it was slack, unprofessional behavior on the job. And lateness was the sign of a sloppy, disorganized schedule.

Involuntarily, Caroline shuddered at the thought of her grandmother's infamous wrath being unleashed upon her. The stern rebuke would be precise, apropos, scathing and delivered with coolly raised, condemnatory eyebrows and in icy tones of haughty grandeur that had in the past reduced many an executive—even the male ones—at Fortune Cosmetics not only to obsequious apologies, but even to tears. Caroline had seen it happen on more than one occasion, although, much to her gratitude and relief, she herself was seldom a target of her grandmother's anger. And she wouldn't be this morning, either, not if she could help it. That would be a disastrous way to start out the new year.

Grabbing her Louis Vuitton totebag and her black leather portfolio from the front passenger seat, Caroline stepped gracefully from the Volvo and slammed the door. The heels of her Maud Frizon pumps clicked briskly on the concrete floor as she hurried toward the bank of elevators that would take her up into the skyscraper owned by her family. As the elevator doors slid open, she rushed down the long, plushly carpeted corridors of one of the hushed upper floors toward the conference room.

By now Caroline had her portfolio open and was leafing through it as she hastened along, reviewing her notes she had prepared for her presentation. So she didn't see Dr. Nicolai Valkov until she literally ran right into him. Like her, he had his head bent over his own portfolio, not watching where he was going. As the two of them collided, both their portfolios and the papers inside went flying. At the unexpected impact, Caroline lost her balance, stumbled, and would have fallen had not Nick's strong, sure hands abruptly shot out, grabbing hold of her and pulling her to him to steady her. She gasped, startled and stricken, as she came up hard against his broad chest, lean hips and corded thighs, her face just inches from his own—as though they were lovers about to kiss.

Caroline had never been so close to Nick Valkov before, and, in that instant, she was acutely aware of him—not just as a fellow employee of Fortune Cosmetics but also as a man. Of how tall and ruggedly handsome he was, dressed in an elegant, pin-striped black suit cut in the European fashion, a crisp white shirt, a foulard tie and a pair of Cole Haan loafers. Of how dark his thick, glossy hair and his deep-set eyes framed by raven-wing brows were—so dark that they were almost black, despite the bright, fluorescent lights that blazed overhead. Of the whiteness of his straight teeth against his bronzed skin as a brazen, mocking grin slowly curved his wide, sensual mouth.

"Actually, I *was* hoping for a sweet roll this morning— but I daresay you would prove even tastier, Ms. Fortune," Nick drawled impertinently, his low, silky voice tinged with a faint accent born of the fact that Russian, not English, was his native language.

At his words, Caroline flushed painfully, embarrassed and annoyed. If there was one person she always attempted to avoid at Fortune Cosmetics, it was Nick Valkov. Following the breakup of the Soviet Union, he had emigrated to the United States, where her grandmother had hired him to direct the company's research and development department. Since that time, Nick had constantly demonstrated marked, traditional, Old World tendencies that had led Caroline to believe he not only had no use for equal rights but also would actually have been more than happy to turn back the clock several centuries where females were concerned. She thought his remark was typical of his attitude toward women: insolent, arrogant and domineering. Really, the man was simply insufferable!

Caroline couldn't imagine what had ever prompted her grandmother to hire him—and at a highly generous salary, too—except that Nick Valkov was considered one of the foremost chemists anywhere on the planet. Deep down inside Caroline knew that no matter how he behaved, Fortune Cosmetics was extremely lucky to have him. Still, that didn't give him the right to manhandle and insult her!

"I assure you that you would find me more bitter than a cup of the strongest black coffee, Dr. Valkov," she insisted, attempting without success to free her trembling body from his steely grip, while he continued to hold her so near that she could feel his heart beating steadily in his chest— and knew he must be equally able to feel the erratic hammering of her own.

"Oh, I'm willing to wager there's more sugar and cream to you than you let on, Ms. Fortune." To her utter mortification and outrage, she felt one of Nick's hands slide insidiously up her back and nape to her luxuriant mass of sable hair, done up in a stylish French twist.

"You know so much about fashion," he murmured, eyeing her assessingly, pointedly ignoring her indignation and efforts to escape from him. "So why do you always wear your hair like this...so tightly wrapped and severe? I've never seen it down. Still, that's the way it needs to be worn, you know...soft, loose, tangled about your face. As it is, your hair fairly cries out for a man to take the pins from it, so he can see how long it is. Does it fall past your shoulders?" He quirked one eyebrow inquisitively, a mocking half smile still twisting his lips, letting her know he was enjoying her obvious discomfiture. "You aren't going to tell me, are you? What a pity. Because my guess is that it does— and I'd like to know if I'm right. And these glasses." He indicated the large, square, tortoiseshell frames perched on her slender, classic nose. "I think you use them to hide behind more than you do to see. I'll bet you don't actually even need them at all."

Caroline felt the blush that had yet to leave her cheeks deepen, its heat seeming to spread throughout her entire quivering body. Damn the man! Why must he be so infuriatingly perceptive?

Because everything that Nick suspected was true.

*   *   *   *   *

To read more, don't miss
HIRED HUSBAND
by Rebecca Brandewyne,
Book One in the new
FORTUNE'S CHILDREN series,
beginning this month and available only from
Silhouette Books!

Who can resist a Texan...or a Calloway?

This September, award-winning author
ANNETTE BROADRICK
returns to Texas, with a brand-new
story about the Calloways...

SONS
→OF←
TEXAS

Rogues and Ranchers

CLINT: The brave leader. Used to keeping secrets.

CADE: The Lone Star Stud. Used to having women
fall at his feet...

MATT: The family guardian. Used to handling
trouble...

They must discover the identity of the mystery
woman with Calloway eyes—and uncover a
conspiracy that threatens their family....

Look for **SONS OF TEXAS:** Rogues and Ranchers
in September 1996!

Only from Silhouette...where passion lives.

Silhouette®

SONSST

MILLION DOLLAR SWEEPSTAKES

Silhouette's recipe for a sizzling summer:

* Take the best-looking cowboy in South Dakota
* Mix in a brilliant bachelor
* Add a sexy, mysterious sheikh
* Combine their stories into one collection and you've got one sensational super-hot read!

Summer Sizzlers

MEN OF Summer

Three short stories by these favorite authors:

Kathleen Eagle
Joan Hohl
Barbara Faith

Available this July wherever
Silhouette books are sold.

Look us up on-line at: http://www.romance.net

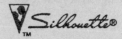

Silhouette®
™

SS96

FORTUNE'S Children™

New York Times Bestselling Author

REBECCA BRANDEWYNE

Launches a new twelve-book series—FORTUNE'S CHILDREN
beginning in July 1996 with Book One

Hired Husband

Caroline Fortune knew her marriage to Nick Valkov was in
name only. She would help save the family business, Nick
would get a green card, and a paper marriage would suit both
of them. Until Caroline could no longer deny the feelings Nick
stirred in her and the practical union turned passionate.

MEET THE FORTUNES—a family whose legacy is greater than
riches. Because where there's a will...there's a wedding!

Look for Book Two, *The Millionaire and the Cowgirl*,
by Lisa Jackson. Available in August 1996 wherever Silhouette
books are sold.

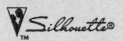

Silhouette®

You're About to Become a *Privileged Woman*

Reap the rewards of fabulous free gifts and benefits with proofs-of-purchase from Silhouette and Harlequin books

Pages & Privileges™

It's our way of thanking you for buying our books at your favorite retail stores.

PROOF OF PURCHASE

SR-PP155

Offer expires October 31, 1996

**Harlequin and Silhouette—
the most privileged readers in the world!**

For more information about Harlequin and Silhouette's PAGES & PRIVILEGES program call the Pages & Privileges Benefits Desk: 1-503-794-2499

Silhouette®

SR-PP155